Whiskers and

♥

KC McCormick Çiftçi

Copyright © 2024 by KC McCormick Çiftçi

All rights reserved.

ISBN: 979-8-9889010-4-4

This is a work of fiction. Names, characters, places, and incidents either are the product of the author's imagination or are used fictitiously. Any resemblance to actual persons, living or dead, events, or locales is entirely coincidental.

No portion of this book may be reproduced in any form without written permission from the publisher or author, except as permitted by U.S. copyright law.

Cover design by Chelsea Kemp.

One

Meredith gave herself one last appraisal in the mirror. She had learned the art of elegant air travel by now. Gone were the days of her youth, showing up for the airport in sweatpants and her hair in a messy bun. As a renowned travel writer, airports, lounges, and first-class cabins were the new boardroom, the new networking event, the sort of places where opportunity could lie around every corner.

You don't want to disqualify yourself for the opportunity when the owner of the next Michelin starred hot spot is passing out invitations, she reminded her reflection. *Which is why you are now the person who needs to hear the announcement that, in the event of a water landing, high heels should be left behind.*

She looked down at her feet, wincing at the way her slingback was already rubbing uncomfortably on the back of her ankle. It was going to be a long day, and she was glad that she would be sitting for most of it.

Meredith made her way down to the lobby of the Hotel Seoul, returning the warm greetings of the staff member who was waiting for her at the front desk. Though there was a twinge of anxiety evident in the voice and mannerisms of the woman—she worked in the travel industry, of course she knew who Meredith Crowne was—she stopped herself from offering anything more than her warmest smile. Years ago, she would have dropped her voice to a whisper and let the young employee know that any mentions of the hotel would be very positive, enjoying it as the nerves visibly melted from the woman's face.

But things were different now, in part because now travel "influencers" would do just that in order to secure a discount, something that Meredith knew was a conflict of interest. Her hesitation to share a reassuring word was also due to the fact that she hadn't yet written a word of her latest piece—that was what travel days were for, in fact—and though she couldn't imagine herself finding anything to critique about the Hotel Seoul, the fact remained that the contents of her piece, from first draft to final draft, were at this point a mystery even to her.

"I'll just let the shuttle driver know that you're ready to leave for the airport, ma'am." The young woman raised her eyebrows in question, her eyes alight with so much hope that Meredith would let something slip, some secret shared between them. "Is that alright?"

"Yes, please." Meredith returned the woman's smile, then stepped away from the counter to wait for the shuttle driver near the hotel's entrance. If she stayed in the hopeful orbit of the desk clerk much longer, her people pleasing tendencies were liable to kick in, reassuring words spilling out of her mouth like the two of them were old friends gossiping in the strictest of confidences.

No, the boundaries Meredith had put in place in her professional life were for her sake as much as they were for anyone else's—*scratch that*, she thought, *they are the greatest, most effective self-care I have ever treated myself to, and I don't care who doesn't like them.*

A few short minutes later, the shuttle appeared in front of the hotel, and with one last wave to the desk clerk, Meredith left the Hotel Seoul for good.

Two

The flight from Seoul to Istanbul was 12 hours long, and Meredith's plan was to spend it typing up her notes about her trip into some semblance of a first draft. She found a quiet spot in the first-class lounge and opened her laptop, checking first to make sure that arrangements for her arrival at the new Istanbul Airport were already in place.

She was booked in the Hotel Begonvil for the next week at least, and scrolling through her inbox, she noted confirmation of her impending arrival, as well as the details of her airport transfer. Everything, it seemed, was in place for a seamless journey from where she sat all the way to the suite where she would be putting up her feet after a long day of travel.

Meredith had travel days down to a science at this point in her career. She could fly through the security line with the best of them, always took time before boarding to do some stretching and lymphatic massage, and she was prepared any day of the week to entertain herself on a long haul flight, even including the potential for delays.

Back when Meredith flew economy, she opted for aisle seats, after discovering on one particularly painful transatlantic flight that she would rather pee on herself than wake the person next to her. Now, though, she didn't have to make tradeoffs like that. She could enjoy the window seat, put her feet up in her first class lounger, and never had to think about things like how long her bladder could tolerate her being immobile.

She settled into her seat as she waited for the rest of the passengers to board, opening up her laptop to begin organizing her notes. Her stomach rumbled, and she reached for the menu card she had been given shortly after boarding. "Oh yum," she mumbled to herself. "Well, I can't say no to my last chance to eat good Korean food for a while."

Three

As the plane completed its final taxi to the gate in Istanbul, Meredith stretched subtly, surveying her surroundings to ensure she had already gathered all of her things. She stifled a yawn and checked the delicate watch on her wrist. It was only 2 pm in Istanbul, but it was 8 pm in Seoul, and her body clock was feeling it.

Flying first class might provide a more comfortable experience than economy—she would always appreciate the ability to spread out and put her feet up, could never take that for granted—but the fact that she opted to spend her travel days writing rather than resting ensured that by the time she arrived at her destination she was still just as exhausted and disoriented as she had been as a 21-year-old snagging the cheapest red eye flight to start her spring break as early as possible.

That the travel bug had bit Meredith had been as much a surprise to her as it had been to her family of teachers. It had begun innocently enough with a summer study abroad program to fulfill her Spanish language requirement. Meredith had even thought at the time that spending a few weeks in Costa Rica would be the perfect way to see the world and prepare her for a life of settling down after graduation. She had even lined up an interview for a part time job at an afterschool tutoring program for her return, eager to put those new Spanish skills to good use.

Of course, things hadn't worked out the way 19-year-old Meredith had expected. Those weeks in Costa Rica had opened her eyes to a wider world, something she hadn't even realized she had been missing, and the idea that she should be satisfied with that taste and not ask for more, while it had made sense to her when she first signed up for the class, was now one of the most laughable moments of her entire youth.

She had canceled the job interview—that had been a necessity, once she had changed her flight home so that she could spend an extra week in Costa Rica—and spent her two remaining semesters researching a new career path, looking for the option that would translate to the greatest amount of time spent seeing the world.

It had been a slog to get from that point to her current one. As she looked out the window of the plane, trying to predict which gate would be the final resting place of their flight, she remembered the first assignments she had taken. Of the cheap flights she had booked, desperately believing that someone, some publication, would want to read—and more importantly, pay her to publish—a piece about her travel experience there.

Because that was often the way it had gone. Despite what she had let her parents believe, she often got paid for her pieces only *after* the trip had been taken. There weren't a lot of publications out there, either in the print world or in the new media realm, that had been looking to take a chance on a green writer fresh out of university, sending her on all expenses paid trips just so the rest of the world could know about the best hotels in Berlin or the hidden spots in Norway.

Now, though, things were different. Meredith had built a reputation that spoke for itself, and the main challenge she faced was juggling the requests of the various high-end publications that bought freelance pieces from her. After all, she couldn't be in two places at once, and she didn't want to commit to only one outlet. The days in which employment felt like security were long gone, and her recent tax returns had proven to her once and for all that betting on herself was the only kind of job security she needed.

As seasoned a traveler as she was, Meredith had airport navigation down to a science. From traveling only with carry-on luggage to purchasing every membership she could get her hands on to skip the lines at passport control and security, she opted for comfort and convenience over saving pennies every time.

Of course, there were some things money couldn't buy. Even though the first class cabin had exited the plane well before everyone else, the line at customs was long enough to take her right back on a trip down memory lane to her early days of traveling.

When she looked back at it now, she could see it for what it was—uncomfortable, exhausting, and, at times, borderline unsafe. But at the time, it had been nothing but thrills and excitement. Though she wouldn't trade in her lounge pass or Global Entry membership for anything, she did miss the awe. It wasn't that she didn't feel awed now;

it was just that it was harder to come by. Her standards had risen with every incredible experience, every landmark she had laid her eyes on after years of vision boarding it, and now it took a little more than a pretty beach or a picturesque line of houses to get her to stop in her tracks.

Meredith pondered the concept as she inched her way through the line. Maybe it was natural, in any line of work, to acclimate with time and exposure and experience. Even to take things for granted. She wondered if veterinarians could still appreciate the cuteness of a puppy or a kitten, if artists were awed by the way the painting took shape with childlike wonder.

But those things are transcendent, she thought. *I should be asking myself if the accountant still gets jazzed about a mess of numbers they get to untangle or if librarians still love…alphabetizing things?* Meredith knew she was being ridiculous, that the daily tasks of her job were anything but mundane and that it was unfair to categorize any job as having less potential for magic. Of *course* librarians loved books, accountants loved numbers, and anyone with the evolutionary impulse to fawn over a baby animal with its big ears, big eyes, and wobbly legs would do just that.

And if Meredith was feeling a little less awed by impressive architecture and natural beauty these days…well maybe Istanbul would cure her of that.

Four

Meredith was staying in the Hotel Begonvil for the duration of her stay in Istanbul, and from the first moment she had made contact, the service had been impressive. She found her shuttle with ease, settling into the comfortable seat with a bottle of chilled sparkling water and enjoying the sounds of some Turkish pop music that the driver leaned forward to turn off as soon as the vehicle started.

"No, it's fine. Please leave it on," she said, noting both his apologetic head nod, as if he had been caught doing something embarrassing, and the warm smile that spread when the two of them—the rest of the shuttle was blissfully empty—relaxed into their seats and the shuttle began moving, the catchy beat propelling them on their way.

The Hotel Begonvil staff welcomed her at the entrance, the boutique hotel festooned with the colorful bougainvillea from which it earned its name. The staff were quick to take her bags, to offer her tea and a place to sit, the very picture of Turkish hospitality. When she was shown to her room, she was greeted by fresh flowers, fine toiletries, and even a selection of Turkish delight.

It was all almost enough to make Meredith break her own rule and let her surprise and delight register on her face—*almost*. But she reminded herself that she was a professional, that beautiful views and soft sheets weren't enough to guarantee a glowing five-star recommendation and that she still had days to enjoy all the hotel had to offer—or for it to let the cracks show, but only time would tell which one it would be.

She also had an entire city to explore, and there was no time to waste on getting started with that.

Left alone to her own devices, after all, she might start wondering what was next after this trip. And if there was one thing Meredith knew, when she was in this sort of headspace, was that it was better to keep moving and not ask those sorts of questions.

She let herself sit on the comfortable chair in her room for two more minutes, closing her eyes and counting her breaths in and out slowly, and then she got to her feet, made her way into the bathroom to wash her hands, dab on just enough makeup to remove the evidence of all the traveling she'd already done that day, and secure her hair in a braid.

Despite all of her "seasoned traveler" bravado, she was abuzz at the idea of finally seeing Istanbul. It was the city most likely to be raved about by her fellow travelers, the one that seemed to have made an impression on everyone who'd set foot there, whether it was for a two-week tour or a 24-hour layover.

"Here goes nothing, then," she murmured to herself as she set off to see what the day held in store for her.

Five

Meredith was in front of the Hotel Begonvil, getting her bearings for her first on-foot exploration. She had, of course, researched the must-see sights in Istanbul, both the mainstream ones and the little known beauties, and she planned to cover them all and also leave plenty of room for serendipity. One never knew what opportunities might present, after all. That was a piece of wisdom that had been imparted on her in her early days of traveling, one fateful day in Prague when she had been prepared to walk her feet bloody to ensure she saw the Astronomical Clock and the Lennon Wall before her midnight flight departed.

"You know," he had told her, "you might actually get to enjoy your travels a bit more if you take a little time to wander and just...you know, see what happens." He had nodded towards the printed itinerary clutched in her hands. "If you treat it like a checklist, you can make it through all the items, take the required selfie in front of each landmark...but to what end? What's the point? Have you actually gotten to feel what the city is like? How the locals live? Or have you simply taken all the right photos to show your friends back home and make them jealous?"

At the time, those comments had infuriated Meredith, and she had let Adnan know he was wrong in no uncertain terms. But when she looked back at that trip now, she could see he had been right. After all, her argument with him, which had begun in the dining room of the hostel where they had both been staying and spilled out into the streets as they walked the Charles Bridge, passing plenty of not-to-be-missed landmarks along the way, had been the most memorable part of the trip.

She hadn't told him she had changed her mind, hadn't wanted to give him the satisfaction. But when they had parted ways that evening—he had insisted on accompanying her on the bus to the airport for some reason she couldn't figure out—an understanding had passed between them.

Meredith had wondered for years if she and Adnan would cross paths again, had looked for him without even realizing she was doing just that in every airport. They hadn't exchanged contact information—or even last names—and the more time went on, the less likely it seemed that they would find themselves in the same place at the same time. After all, Adnan was a "go with the flow" traveler, and even if his philosophy had rubbed off on her just a little—enough to make her keep an afternoon or two free for serendipity, but not to abandon her entire itinerary—she doubted they were running in the same circles these days. Adnan was probably still a frequent hostel stayer, while Meredith was all about comfort and luxury.

She was thinking of him as she walked from the hotel to the center of Sultanahmet, where some of the most quintessentially Istanbul landmarks awaited. She would never hear the end of it if she finally made it to this city without at least visiting the Hagia Sophia and the Blue Mosque, and as disinclined as she normally was to fall for the appeal of the most famous sights, she had a sneaking suspicion that she wouldn't be let down.

And perhaps it was because Adnan was already on her mind that when she first came into view of the Blue Mosque and stopped to take in the architectural wonder that she didn't even notice, didn't even balk at the familiar face of the tour guide who was explaining the history of its construction to a group of tourists.

"Notice the six minarets? That's a few more than normal, isn't it? Well, according to the story, that was all due to a misunderstanding because the words for *gold* and *six* sound a bit similar in Turkish..." His words were flowing to her ears, washing over her but not exactly sinking in, as if a podcast were continuing to play in her ears while she was lost in thought. She would have to skip back a few times to pick up the thread where she had lost it...

...but this was real life, not a podcast. And the words were coming from a man she hadn't seen in years and wasn't even sure she was really seeing now.

He looked older than she remembered, his hair still dark but the evidence of years, wisdom, and maybe even a touch of maturity written on his features. There were just the beginnings of creases at the corners of his eyes, further confirmation that he was, in fact, the same Adnan she had met in Prague—that man, after all, had always been ready with a smile.

Meredith hadn't even realized that she had been staring at him, not until his eyes landed on her and his explanation trailed off.

"Right," he said to the tourists who were milling around him, seemingly anxious to be set free to explore on their own. "Why don't you all take the next thirty minutes to walk around outside and we'll meet here again and go inside together?"

His eyes hadn't left hers since he had first spotted her, and yet as the group dispersed, she was ready to bolt. She could join them, snapping some photos of the outside of the 17th century structure and jotting down some notes from his monologue to double check later.

But the crowd had thinned and before she could think twice about it, Adnan was in front of her and her heart was racing. Maybe it wasn't even him. Maybe this was his doppelgänger, and he was only coming to talk to her because he had caught her tagging along on his tour without paying for it. Yes, that had to be it.

She put up a hand in a placating gesture before he could even begin speaking. "I was just moving on," she said. "I caught the tail end of your explanation about the minarets but don't worry, I'm not trying to be a tour parasite and hang on."

Adnan—or at least, this man who sure looked like Adnan—was smiling and shaking his head. "Meredith? Is that really you? I know I haven't seen you in eight years, but I swear if that isn't you, I'll..." He looked around as if searching for the end of his sentence. "I'll eat my hat. I think people used to say that, though it makes less sense now, considering." He gestured towards his hatless head. "Is that really you? Or have I embarrassed myself with a Meredith lookalike?"

Despite herself, she smiled at him. "It's really me. And is it really you, Adnan? I was just convincing myself of the same thing, in fact. That you must be Adnan's doppelgänger or else an identical twin that you never bothered to tell me about."

Adnan threw his head back as a laugh roared out of him. "Why didn't I even consider the twin angle? But then you'd say, all innocently, that no, you aren't Meredith's twin and then in the end it would turn out that the two of you are in fact triplets and there's even another woman with that face wandering around in the world!"

She had to laugh at him. "You should either write soap operas or stop watching so many of them." She craned her neck to track the length of the minarets. "This is a pretty incredible building. So you do tours now? What else have you been up to in the last eight years?" She caught a part of herself wanting to ask him if he was married, in a relationship, settled down, a parent...but was relieved when none of those questions came out of her mouth.

"Yes, it's great, isn't it? I've been doing tours for a while now, mostly in Istanbul, but sometimes I get a group that's exploring more of Turkey, and then I travel with them down the coast or to some of the archaeological sites further east. I'm having a blast doing it. What about you?" He gave her a quick once-over, taking in her backpack, blouse, and tailored trousers. "Why do I feel like you're a high-end Indiana Jones?"

Meredith chuckled at that. "Well, you aren't far off. I'm a travel writer now, but doing things a bit differently than when we met back in Prague. It's more luxury hotels and high-end experiences these days than dorm beds in hostels and bargain hunting."

"Very nice," said Adnan with a sincere nod. "That fits with what I remember about you, and it seems like you're doing well for yourself." While he was talking a small calico cat had approached them and begun twining itself around his legs.

Meredith recoiled, pointing at the cat. "There's, uh...do you want that rubbing itself on your legs like that? I mean, who knows what it has, what kind of fleas or diseases or..."

Her words trailed off as the cat stood on its hind legs, its front legs pawing at Adnan's thigh. When he crouched down ever so slightly, the cat leaped, landing first on his back and then climbing up to Adnan's shoulder, where it peered down at Meredith from a height.

She couldn't help herself, she shrieked. "What the—?"

Adnan grinned as he looked up at the cat on his shoulder. "Meredith, this is Poppy. Poppy, this is Meredith."

Six

"Right, so." Meredith was tight-lipped, looking up at the cat and barely stopping herself from sneering at it. "Clearly you two are already acquainted and you seem to have no concern about fleas or any other sort of vermin."

Adnan smiled, reaching up with one hand to stroke the cat, who leaned into the open palm, closing its eyes and purring. "Poppy is my travel companion. My co-worker. I suppose you could call her my life partner, though that does make our relationship sound a bit more romantic than it actually is." He looked up at the cat, who was kneading its paws on his shoulder. "It's not that I don't love you though, buddy. You know I do. But we're more like pals. Best friends. And she's the best wingman when I'm trying to impress a lady."

Meredith pulled her lips into her mouth, stopping herself from saying something. She wanted to question what kind of woman, exactly, would be impressed by an animal so prone to carrying diseases or which was inclined to gift its favorite humans small dead animals, but it was clear from the mutual affection between Adnan and Poppy that her question wouldn't win her any points.

"Well, I should let you get back to your tour," she said, ducking her head. "It really was great to run into you."

"You, too." Adnan's eyes lingered on her face as she watched something dawn in his expression. "But wait...you're in Istanbul for a few days at least, right?" When she nodded, his smile grew. "Then we should meet up again! Let me show you around. What are you doing tonight? For dinner? Could I take you out?"

She hesitated. She was here to experience the city, to document it in a way that would make would-be travelers want to book their own flights. She was not there to rekindle a potential romance or wonder about the one that got away...

"I'll take you somewhere nearby, with a great view and even better food," Adnan offered, his smile taking on a forced quality that hadn't been there before. "It'll be perfect for whatever you're writing about Istanbul."

That settled it. Meredith nodded. "Can you meet me in front of the Hotel Begonvil? That's where I'm staying."

"Perfect. I'll pick you up there at seven."

"Great. Will...um, will Poppy be joining us?" Without realizing what she was doing, she reached toward the cat, surprised when it leaned forward to meet her hand, rubbing its forehead against her palm with a force that nearly threw her off balance.

Adnan shook his head. "She's not much for night life. Or rather, the restaurants in Istanbul tend to come with their own cats and they frown on you bringing your own. It's a bit like showing up with your own bottle of wine.

So Poppy will stay at home with a nice bowl of cat food, a little catnip, and a video of mice or birds or fish on the iPad to keep her company. Don't worry about her."

I wasn't, thought Meredith, though she was still petting the cat. *I asked because I didn't want to spend more time with her, and yet why am I still petting the thing?*

It was at that moment that she realized how close she was standing to Adnan, how with her arm raised to pet Poppy, it was almost as if the two of them were about to embrace.

Mystery solved, I guess. This might be the reason I can't stop petting Poppy. Don't take it personally, Poppy. This doesn't make me a cat lover.

As if Poppy was reading her thoughts, she got up from her perch on Adnan's shoulder and took one step forward and down, leaving Meredith shocked into silence with her mouth wide open as the cat once again took a seat, this time on her shoulder.

"What in the—?" She tentatively lowered her hand until it touched Poppy's whiskered head, just a few inches above her shoulder.

Adnan was grinning broadly. "She likes you! She never gets on anyone else's shoulder. Hang on, can I take a picture? I want to remember this."

She nodded, but she was still more or less frozen in place as Adnan raised his phone and snapped a picture. She was vaguely aware of him telling her to smile and of the grimace that was her best attempt at following the command.

When Poppy started purring, she felt her eyes go wide. Was it always that loud when a cat purred? Or was there something wrong with her, like maybe something had come loose inside and that's why she was rattling so loudly?

"She's a loud purrer, isn't she?" Adnan asked, stepping towards her to scratch Poppy behind the ears. He tapped his own shoulder. "Come on, girl, come back over here. Leave Meredith alone so she can get on with her day."

No, that's okay, she thought, a part of her hating the thought of her empty, cold shoulder when Poppy's warm body was gone. "Thanks," she said instead, forcing a smile. She dusted off her shoulder when Poppy was back on Adnan's shoulder. The part of her that still thought cats were dirty animals was itching to get back to the hotel and send her button-down shirt straight off to the hotel laundry.

"I'll see you at seven," she said, her eyes darting up to Poppy for just a second. "And see you...around, I guess, Poppy?"

Poppy gave her a slow blink, and Adnan gifted her a smile to match. "I should get back to my group," said Adnan, "but I'm already looking forward to tonight. It's really so great to see you again, and I can't wait to catch up on everything we've missed."

Meredith swallowed, surprising herself with how strongly she related to his words. "Me, too."

Though they parted ways, neither of them left the courtyard. Adnan returned to his tour group, and Meredith tried to give them space, not wanting to continue to bump into her old potential flame, to make the same smiles they would if they were colleagues who crossed paths three times in quick succession in the same hallway. When the tour group ventured inside the mosque, she remained outside, continuing to snap photos and jot down notes and a few questions to ask Adnan later—what was the point of having dinner with a tour guide if not to get some inside scoop?

But even as she wondered that, she knew it wasn't reality at all. Part of her might be trying to justify her upcoming dinner as information gathering, as doing her due diligence to write the best possible piece about the city she was currently exploring. But even if a small part of her was making that justification, there was a much larger part of her that knew she was having dinner with Adnan only because she wanted to. Only because her heart had picked up its pace when her eyes had landed on him and because the flood of memories of the time they had shared had been nothing but warm and enticing and filled with possibility.

Because she could admit it to herself now, even if she hadn't been able to eight years ago: there had been a spark. Hell, there still was a spark, if she was interpreting her own feelings accurately and she wasn't misreading anxiety as attraction. Maybe Adnan always made eye contact with people like he was peering into their souls, but it sure felt like something special was transpiring between them. It was as if, when their eyes were locked on each other, there was an entire conversation happening apart from the surface level pleasantries that their mouths were speaking.

They were saying *I missed you* and *I always wondered what could have been* and *it can't merely be coincidence that we're finding each other again*.

She knew he had reentered the courtyard before she even turned, felt him there like a phantom limb. As she turned on the spot, her eyes were drawn to his across the crowd as naturally as if he had called her name. She smiled at him, a sigh escaping her throat with something like relief at being in the same space as him again.

It felt like she was in trouble. Like she was teetering on the edge of something, about to lose her balance in the sort of way that might have devastating consequences.

And yet there was nothing she could do to stop it. She knew she wouldn't even dream of canceling her date with Adnan, that she couldn't bear the agony of wondering what might have been if she didn't spend as much time with him as she possibly could.

With that thought in mind, she nodded once, then turned on her heel to return to the hotel to begin preparing for the evening ahead.

Seven

When Meredith exited the Hotel Begonvil for the second time that day, Adnan was waiting for her with a smile on his face and a single rose in his hand. She cocked her head, looking meaningfully at the rose.

Adnan rubbed the back of his neck, a hint of embarrassment coloring his cheeks. "Ah yes, this," he said. "When I was walking over, someone was selling them. The usual tourist thing, you know. Looking for couples and then applying a little guilt and pressure until one of them buys a flower for the other one. But it made me aware that I wanted to make it very clear to you that, in my eyes at least, this is a date. And so I got you a flower." He lifted one hand to toy with the petals on the rose. "I am realizing now, though, that this is now something you will have to carry around for the evening." He finally met her eyes. "If you would prefer to take it and leave it in your hotel room, that is fine with me."

Meredith gave him what she hoped was a reassuring smile. She couldn't help but notice that he had skipped right over his assertion of their being on a date. "I will carry it proudly on our date." She extended a hand to him, and he placed the rose in it. She let her arm drop, play acting as if the weight of the flower was unexpectedly heavy. "Oh, just kidding," she said. "I don't think I have the strength." She straightened up, shaking her head at him, as she tucked the rose into the side of her large purse so that it was peeking out but unlikely to be damaged as they navigated the crowds. "Thank you, Adnan. It's lovely."

"I'm glad you like it." He offered his arm to her, and she tucked her hand into the crook of his elbow, letting him guide her away from the hotel. "It's been quite some time since I took someone on a date, so as soon as I bought the rose I was second guessing myself and doubting it was the cool thing to do. I almost chucked it in the trash more times than I care to admit."

She shook her head at him. "Now that would have been ridiculous. Surely you could have at least pawned it off on someone else rather than throwing it away." She smiled, warmed from within at the revelation that Adnan was a bit rusty in the dating department. "I haven't been on a date in a long time either," she offered as a means of reassurance, "So I'm definitely not judging. Far from an expert in this department."

When she glanced up at Adnan, he was smiling. "I'm glad. Both that you aren't judging me and that the stars have aligned to have us both single in the moment we meet again. There's nothing worse than reconnecting with the one that got away only to find out they're engaged, married, or have joined the priesthood."

Meredith laughed despite herself. "You have a lot of experience in that department?"

His eyes were serious when they found hers. "Not at all. Apart from you, I mean. I've just seen enough Turkish dramas to know how things could have worked out."

"Ah." She nodded. Then they both fell into silence, walking comfortably until they arrived at an unassuming restaurant with a view of the Bosphorus.

"This is lovely," Meredith breathed as they arrived at the terrace, taking in the view.

"I was hoping you would like it. That it would make an impression."

Meredith took a seat as Adnan pulled out her chair for her and then pushed it toward the table. "Something to write about in my Istanbul piece, you mean?"

He took the seat across from hers. She couldn't help but notice that while she had a great view of the lights reflecting on the water, all Adnan could see was her. "You can come sit next to me," she offered before he could answer her question. "So you can enjoy the view too, I mean."

He shook his head, smiling at her. "I'm quite happy with my view, actually. Thank you, though." He looked over his shoulder, taking in the view. "And to answer your question, I didn't have this place in mind specifically so that your piece about Istanbul would include the best restaurants and hidden gems." He turned back to face her. "I just thought you would like it. And when was the last time you approached a city in terms of what is enjoyable to you and not what is going to be the best for your legion of loyal readers?"

Her face heated at the truth in his words, at the implication that he was aware of the scope of her writing career. "Luckily," she began, taking a sip of water, "my readers and I tend to like the same things. It's not as if I'm putting myself out experiencing the best dining and most unique sights each city I visit has to offer."

Adnan's smile was smaller now, deferential. "Of course. I only mean that...well, I think of that day that we spent in Prague, how we just walked around freely and let the city surprise us. The things we didn't expect to see that were the best part, the food we ate from some little hole in the wall restaurant. It's hard to have an experience like that when, in the back of your mind at least, you know people are going to be reading your words with a certain expectation. That you might very well be creating the itinerary for their next vacation."

Meredith pursed her lips and nodded as she contemplated his words. "Believe it or not, I did actually learn something from that day we spent together all those years ago. When I come to a new city, I have my list of must see, must do, must experience things...but I also keep an afternoon free to just wander and let serendipity happen. In honor of your way of doing things, I guess."

Adnan widened his eyes in mock horror. "Wow, a whole afternoon without a fixed agenda? You're really quite a daredevil, you know?" He chuckled then. "I'm just teasing you, of course. And I'm glad that you have some free time built in to just see what happens. Of course I wish it was more, but I get it. Your readers might revolt if your next piece was, 'sorry y'all, but I didn't actually see much of Madrid besides my hotel room and the convenience store. I was feeling unmotivated and homesick, so I just ate snacks and watched Spanish television. Can't say I recommend it since you can have the same experience—but actually understand the TV—if you just stay at home.'"

The menu slipped from Meredith's fingers, landing on the table. "First of all," she breathed between laughs, "I have never used the word *y'all* in my writing, speaking, or anywhere else. And of course I wouldn't spend a weekend in Madrid lying in my hotel room eating snacks. When you've paid to travel somewhere, isn't it, like, your obligation to see as much of it as you can?"

He tilted his head to the side as if conceding—but only slightly—to her point. "Maybe. But I am not much of a believer in FOMO and I really love my sleep. So if I'm feeling a little sick or just sleepy, then I'm going to sleep as much as I possibly can, even if there's a damn parade happening outside my room's window. I might need some earplugs, but I'm going to take care of myself."

Meredith had picked the menu back up and was studying it, looking for things on her "list of foods to try in Istanbul" list before she would ask Adnan for a recommendation. After all, she had planned to navigate this and all meals alone, and it wouldn't do to let him take over her plans for the evening—or for the days ahead, though she knew she was getting ahead of herself wondering just how much time he would want to spend together.

When the silence between them had lapsed long enough to nearly touch the edge of being awkward, she spoke again. "I guess you've grown up since Prague, too."

"How do you mean?" He was studying her, his long fingers drumming on the edge of the menu.

She shrugged. "I mean it in much the same way I've grown up, I guess. No more sleeping in hostels, barely eating a vegetable for weeks at a time, staying up almost all night fueled by just the right proportions of alcohol and caffeine and then jumping out of bed bright and early for the next adventure."

Adnan shuddered. "No, that all sounds terrible to me now. I think that's just growing up, though. Now I'm an old man with a cat who expects me to be home at the same time every evening to feed her dinner. And I know if I stay out late, I'll be hearing complaints from my neighbors about all the meowing while she roams around the apartment looking for me." He looked down, shaking his head with a sigh. "It's tough being a single father, but it's worth it to see my little girl grow up happy and healthy."

That got a laugh out of Meredith. "I guess parenting will do that." She paused, chewing her lip as a thought occurred to her. "So you aren't really traveling as much anymore? I mean, I guess you can't since someone has to put the baby to bed every night..."

Adnan's grin was bright. "Oh, I'm traveling all over Turkey. You saw how Poppy was today, right? She's like the best sidekick and colleague and companion, all rolled up into one. To be fair, she hasn't tried flying on an airplane yet, so I don't know how much of the rest of the world is available to us to explore, but for right now at least, we both are more than happy to see all Turkey has to offer."

"I'd love some recommendations. This is my first trip to Turkey, but if you say there are other cities I need to visit, then I guess I'll be back." Meredith plowed ahead, the pang of envy she had felt towards Poppy better left stifled than explored. "Even if you and I clearly have different ideas of the right way to travel, I'm the last one to question your taste. You did sing Christmas carols in March with me at Wenceslas Square in Prague, after all."

That got her a laugh. "Hey, I hardly think the fact that you're a type A traveler and I'm a type B traveler makes us incompatible. For traveling together, I mean." Adnan was studying the menu now, not making eye contact. "We should think about what to order. Before the waiter comes, I mean. Is there anything in particular you want to try? Or any dietary restrictions I should be aware of?"

Meredith shook her head. "I eat everything. Rather, I try to eat a little bit of everything when I travel, in fact, so that I can share more recommendations with my readers. It wouldn't make sense to just find the one thing I love most and eat it over and over again, so..." She pulled out her phone and began thumbing through her notes. "I have written down that I should eat some fish and lots of kebabs and something called a 'wet burger,' but I actually might have to draw a line there because the name is really just one of the more unappetizing combinations of words out there..." She trailed off, hesitant to say more out of fear she had just insulted Adnan's favorite food.

He had reached across the table to pull down the top of her menu, waiting for her eyes to find his. "Do you mean to tell me," he began, when she at last dared to make eye contact, "that you even decide what to eat based on what other people are going to like? Do you ever wonder if, in your quest to have the broadest appeal to your fanbase, you miss out on so much? Where is the authenticity, Meredith? Surely, pursuing your heart's desire is going to yield a more interesting itinerary than trying to plan the perfect trip that anyone is going to enjoy." He huffed out a laugh, but there was no humor in it. "I mean, have you met most people, Mer? Because I work with tourists daily, and I can tell you that they broadly fall into two camps: those who are in awe of every single little thing they see or experience, and those who can find fault in every single little thing. If you try to make both of those groups of people happy, one will be thrilled every time and one is never going to give you the time of day. Why not simply enjoy yourself?"

Meredith blinked rapidly at Adnan. *This was all a bit much, wasn't it? Too intense for a first date, even if there was nothing that felt "first" about it. It was more like they were picking back up a conversation that had lapsed into silence eight years ago.* "Have I done anything to give you the impression that I'm not enjoying myself?" she asked finally, taking a sip of water. "Because as much as I enjoy your insights, they're feeling a little heavy on the unwanted advice, and that's the one thing that I have a rule about not consuming, no matter where I am."

Adnan sighed, his expression softening. "You're right. God, you're totally right." He reached up to scratch his chin. "I'm acting like we're the same people we were eight years ago, back before our frontal lobes were finished developing. And while it might be tolerable to listen to a 23-year-old man wax on about all that he knows about life, I guess it's less cute when the guy is 31."

Meredith tilted her head to the side, studying him. "It's never really cute. It's just that younger women are more willing to smile and nod along and pretend your insights are ground breaking. This side of 30, I don't have time for that."

He laughed then. "Fair enough. Here's to being on the better side of 30, then." He lifted his water glass up and clinked it with hers.

When the waiter returned, Adnan grimaced at Meredith. "Do you trust me to order?" he asked. "Since we didn't actually get around to figuring out what to get and since"—he gestured around them at the busy restaurant, the waiter who already seemed to be antsy to move on to his next table—"if we don't strike while the iron is hot, we'll end up eating cold, wet burgers or whatever the saying is."

She gestured deferentially towards him, waving at the menu. "By all means, go crazy. Just...well, it should go without saying, but please order Turkish food. I can't very well write about pesto pasta or chicken tikka masala in my Istanbul piece."

With a nod, Adnan got to work, speaking with the waiter for the next moments and gesturing to different areas on the menu. When he was finished and the menus had been cleared away, he graced Meredith with a warm smile.

"Do you want to know what I ordered, or do you want to be surprised?"

She thought about it for just a moment before nodding. "Surprised, please. It's not often that I get the chance to be surprised these days, at least not in a good way, so I'll take it when the opportunity presents."

"The bad surprises are definitely not the highlights of the trip, then? You don't have to spin everything, gaslight yourself into thinking there's a silver lining to every flight delay?"

She shook her head. "Every flight delay, every landmark that is closed for restoration, every flash storm that keeps me stuck in the hotel. I mean, I can tell myself that...I don't know, it's the universe protecting me from some unfortunate incident or whatever..." She shrugged. "But even if that's true, it makes my job harder when a trip is cut short or the planned stops get messed up. It always works out in the end, but not before causing me a little extra stress every time."

"I can see how that would be the case." The waiter had arrived with two glasses of red wine, and Adnan lifted his now, gesturing for her to do the same. "Can I make a toast?"

She nodded. "Of course."

"Well." He took a slow breath with a long exhale, smiling at her for an uncomfortably long time. "Even if serendipity isn't real and everything is just a coincidence...Meredith, here's to our paths crossing again today. To being in the same place at the same time, out of all the other places we could have been. Not just in Istanbul, I mean, though there are certainly plenty of them here. But..." He paused, shaking his head. "The entire world, Mer. You could have come to the Blue Mosque half an hour later or decided today was the right day to cruise across the Bosphorus or even just gone right across the way to the Hagia Sophia instead. We could have missed each other so easily. But we didn't. And I, for one, think that is special and important and not something I can dismiss easily. I'm glad you're back in my life."

When he leaned forward with his glass, she mirrored his gesture, unable to find words to respond to his confession.

Instead, she took a long sip of the wine, its dryness pulling in her cheeks in a delightful way.

"It's good," she said, nodding towards the glass as she replaced it on the table. "And thank you for the toast. I'm glad to be back in the same space as you, too."

The smile he gave her contained so much mischief she had to tear her eyes away from it. "So," he began, twirling the stem of his wine glass on the table and studying it like it was the most interesting thing he'd ever seen, "was it the same for you as it was for me?"

"How so?" she asked, frowning. It wasn't as if she had the first idea how he had spent the last eight years.

"I mean..." He lifted his eyes to hers. "Did you always wonder about me? About what might have been? Was I 'the one that got away'?" He used his fingers to make air quotes around the phrase. "When you heard a Taylor Swift song, one of the sad ones, not one of the angry ones, was I the person you thought of?"

She chuckled at his last question, thinking of all the times she had sung along to "Back to December" with him in mind, conveniently overlooking the fact that they'd actually spent a day together in March. "Maybe," she admitted. The two sips of wine she had drunk combined with the awareness that she and Adnan had a maximum of seven days together before she would be leaving Istanbul. "What's the point of pining after someone if you're not going to at least...I don't know...look them up on social media and try to reconnect?"

Adnan raised an eyebrow at her. "Do you mean to tell me that you know my last name and still didn't do just that? Because rest assured, if I had known yours, I would have been sending you a Facebook friend request back when that was still the cool thing to do. It was only when I stumbled onto one of your *Wanderlust* pieces a couple years ago—or when I saw the author photo attached to it, more specifically—that I knew who you were. Of course, that didn't exactly do me any good, considering you never responded to my message."

Meredith frowned. "You never sent me a message."

"I most certainly did." He nodded. "Probably about two years ago now."

She was already fumbling for her phone. "I swear you didn't. A text message? I would have responded to that, after you convinced me that you were a real person I actually knew and not just a catfish or a real-life phishing scam. Where did you send it?"

"It was on Instagram. Where, I couldn't help but notice, you have quite a few followers." He grimaced. "And where, I'm now realizing, you primarily reshare your own publications. Can't say I've ever seen so much as a personal story posted there."

Meredith returned his grimace. "Right. That's because my sister runs my Instagram account." She held up her phone to show him the home page of her Instagram feed. "See? I have the app, but I never even use it." She tapped over to the direct messages and then showed him the unread messages waiting there. "I don't bother with these, and I tell Callie not to either." She handed him her phone. "Find your profile for me. At least then I can follow you back."

"Even if that's the worst possible way for the two of us to stay in touch, judging by the '99+' unread messages there."

Still, he took her phone from her outstretched hand and, after typing quickly on the screen, handed it back to her, his own profile staring back at her.

Sure enough, the blue button under his brief bio read "Follow back" and Meredith tapped it with no small feeling of guilt. The awareness that she and Adnan could have reconnected years before stung, bringing the feeling that she had missed out, that she had wasted time, that she had lost something she could never get back. She looked at his profile for just a moment longer, noting a collection of artistic photos of Istanbul landmarks, most of them featuring Poppy front and center. Naturally, because humans on the internet liked nothing more than a cute cat, he had racked up a decent following of his own, which made her feel even worse for having missed him here.

When she looked up, replacing her phone in her purse, Adnan was looking at his own phone, a deep frown creasing his forehead.

"Is everything okay?"

He shook his head. "No, not really. It's my neighbor, texting to say that Poppy got into her apartment somehow and now she can't go back home." He sighed. "I knew I shouldn't have left the balcony open, but she likes to sit out there and watch the birds and I figured I would be the only one paying the price later, when I'd have to kill a few mosquitoes that invariably ended up inside."

Meredith pulled her lower lip into her mouth. "So she climbed from your balcony onto the neighbor's balcony? What floor do you live on, anyway? That sounds scary."

Adnan nodded. "Oh, I skipped over that part because I didn't want to have a full-on panic attack at dinner. But yeah, we're up on the fourth floor. Not as high as we could be, but still high enough to get into some serious trouble. The little daredevil should know better than that, but from the sounds of it, my neighbor was cooking fish and so I'm sure Poppy didn't even give it a second thought."

Meredith pushed back her chair and reached for her purse. "We should go. I'm sure Poppy is scared, being in an unfamiliar place, and I'm also sure it won't do any favors for your relationship with your neighbor if she's trying to eat fish in peace with a cat circling her feet begging like she's never once in her life been fed."

He gestured for her to sit down, but she could see the hesitation in his eyes. "Really? No. We can't do that. It's your first night in Istanbul, and you should have a nice meal out, enjoying all the city has to offer. Poppy will be fine, and I'll make it up to my neighbor somehow."

But Meredith was already on her feet, gesturing for the waiter's attention. "Why don't we just see if they can box up the meal to go? I think I'd feel more relaxed—and I know you would—if no one was worrying about Poppy and her safety."

If she had wondered if Adnan would resist, continuing to insist that there was no need to cut the evening short, she had her answer as she watched the relief wash over his face. "I'll make it up to you," he said as he got to his feet as well, stepping towards the approaching waiter. "I promise."

Eight

♥♥
♥

It didn't take long before the meals were packed, the bill was paid, and they were ready to go. While they had waited, Meredith had increased the size of the sips she took from her wineglass, the one thing that wouldn't be joining them when they left the restaurant. Adnan was occupied, first attending to the questions of the waiter and then firing off a series of text messages with his neighbor.

Meredith, meanwhile, sipped her wine and wondered about the cocktail of emotions she was feeling. There was a part of her wondering who, exactly, Adnan's neighbor was and what the nature of the relationship was. Was his concern solely about Poppy, or was there, perhaps, something brewing between the two of them that would make him especially concerned about her comfort level?

She took another pull from her wineglass, cringing inwardly at the thought. Who was she to make any kind of claim on Adnan? And what did she care if there was someone in his life with whom he enjoyed some flirtation or lived out his own personal "will they won't they" sitcom relationship dynamic? And was she even going to examine the fact that she had been the one to insist they return to the apartment and collect Poppy? Since when was she a cat lover? Since when was the thought of someone's pet being locked out of their own home the kind of thing that made her so uncomfortable she simply had to spring into action?

Maybe it had begun when she had met Poppy that very day, when the tiny but feisty beast had perched on Meredith's shoulder, her tail tickling the back of her neck. It had certainly increased exponentially as she had observed her with Adnan, and then again when she had caught a glimpse of his social media and the sheer quantity of photos of his cat. No, it would be clear to anyone with even the most rudimentary levels of empathy that Adnan's first love was his cat and that his concern for her safety would have colored the rest of the evening.

Plus, this way I get to see where he lives, thought Meredith, pulling her lips into her mouth as she recalled that also meant she would be meeting the neighbor that Adnan was currently texting.

"Sorry," he said, looking up at her at last. "Poppy is a bit stressed, and Celia has a cat of her own, and it's all a bit of a mess. There isn't much I can do about it from here, but..." He held up his phone and shrugged. "Well, I'm trying."

Meredith nodded. "It's good that we're going, then. Poppy will be back home soon, and your neighbor won't have to keep worrying about her for much longer. She sounds like a nice person, though, to be helping an animal like that even when it's probably putting a real damper on her evening."

"She's a very nice person." Adnan nodded. "A great neighbor, too. The kind who shares her cooking when it's something extra tasty...but also the kind who understands and appreciates boundaries." He pulled a face then. "I'm going to have to work on Poppy about that. Because climbing into someone's window and asking them to share their dinner is pretty much the exact opposite of having nice, respectful boundaries in place, isn't it?"

Meredith chuckled. "I mean...I know different cultures have different understandings of what is an appropriate level of interaction between neighbors or between family members even...but yeah. Climbing in the window with the aim of sneaking a fish off someone's stove is probably the kind of behavior that only happens in folk tales to teach a lesson to the kids listening to them."

He hung his head. "And it's never the hero of the tale doing it, is it? No, this is the kind of behavior that earns you the punishment of having a spell cast on you by the town wizard." He lifted his head to look into Meredith's eyes, a hint of humor shining there for the first time since he had received his neighbor's message. "Should she be put in solitary confinement as punishment for her bad behavior? Turned into a newt, perhaps? Do you know any wizards?"

"I'm pretty sure by the time we see Poppy, she will have no idea why she's at your neighbor's house, and no memory at all of her misbehavior, so I can't imagine it would be a very effective punishment." She sighed. "It does sound like she should be grounded, though. No unsupervised balcony time, and probably no screen time either, if you want to be a strict parent about it."

Adnan's laugh was so quiet, barely more than a breath, that she felt herself pulled forward to hear it. "I suppose next you'll tell me no boyfriends, no going to the mall with her friends." He sucked in a breath, then shook his head. "We'll play it 'good cop, bad cop' then, okay? You'll be, like, the strict parent I guess, and I'll be the cool, easy, breezy one."

Meredith pulled back. "Uh..." she sputtered, unable to find her next words. "I mean, I..."

But Adnan was already shaking his head. "Sorry. I knew as soon as I said it that it was too much. I'm not actually intending to propose to you, ask you to co-parent my naughty cat. It came out wrong." He leaned forward, reaching for her hand. "Forget I said it, okay?"

She nodded, feeling her cheeks heat with the awareness that part of her, at least, didn't mind the thought of co-parenting a cat with Adnan. *Well, it wasn't the co-parenting of it all that I was excited by, now was it?*

The waiter returned then with their food and a portable credit card machine, sparing her from having to examine her feelings any further, and even worse, from expressing them to Adnan.

She put up a brief fight when he went to pay the bill, suggesting that they should split it, but at the look of offense he gave her and his firm insistence that it had always been his intention to treat her to dinner and that she should really worry about her own business, she relented with a laugh.

"Okay then, the next one will be on me."

He looked up from the machine where he was tapping his card for a contactless transaction, a heat in his eyes that she hadn't seen before—no, that wasn't entirely true; she had seen it in Prague. "I'm going to hold you to that." He blinked twice in quick succession. "It's not about the free meal, of course. But the thought that I'm going to get to see you again before you leave." He slipped his card back into his wallet, exchanged a quick word with the waiter, and got to his feet, offering her a hand. "You just say the word and I'll be ready anytime."

Nine

The taxi to Adnan's apartment was short enough, with most of the traffic headed in the opposite direction at that hour. They got out a short walk away, an assortment of one-way streets making the drive longer than the walk would have been. He insisted on carrying the food, though, as there were two bags—had they really ordered that much?—he deigned to give her the smaller one so that he could keep his elbow free for her to hold onto.

"This is a nice neighborhood," said Meredith, looking around at the buildings that seemed to have been there for generations. "It seems like..." She trailed off, unsure how to express her question in a way that didn't sound like she doubted tour guiding was the most lucrative business out there.

"Like it's probably expensive to live here and you're not sure how I can afford it?" Adnan asked with a good-natured smile. "It's a family house. My parents live here most of the year, but in the summer they head to the southern coast of Turkey, preferring to enjoy the hot weather in a place where they can swim in the sea and relax with their fellow retirees. We switch places then. When they come to Istanbul, I head down to Didim."

"Oh!" Again, she fumbled for the right words. "Do you...not get along with your parents?"

At that, Adnan laughed. "Well, it's not as if I'm avoiding them. They know I'm here, and we do spend time in the same city regularly. It's just better for all of us..." He winced. "It's better for me to have a little of my own space. I'm sure they would like to have me around all the time, but I'm not exactly interested in regressing right back to my childhood and letting my mom do my laundry and cook all my meals for me."

They had arrived at a tall, homey looking building, and Adnan opened the surrounding gate to let them in. She barely took in the building's details as she followed him through the garden, in the front door and up to the fourth floor. It wasn't often that she visited a home on her travels, though she was no stranger to the best hotels every city had to offer. There was something comforting, something almost cozy about being in this environment, about being in a real building where people really lived.

Meredith barely stopped herself from snorting at the thought, grateful that she hadn't spoken it out loud. Was it really such an incredible feat to see a *real building* where *real people* lived? Had she ever met a person who wasn't real? And wasn't every city in the world full of homes, offices, grocery stores, and every other sort of normal building that existed?

Approaching a door, Adnan handed the bag of food to Meredith and then lifted his hand to knock. A man opened the door, his face spreading with a broad smile at the sight of the two of them. "Adnan!" he cried before calling back over his shoulder. "It's Adnan. Tell Poppy her dad is here to pick her up."

Before Meredith could wonder too much at the fact that the man was speaking English, he turned his attention to her. "Hi," he said, holding out a hand for her to shake. "You must be Meredith. I'm Enes. It's nice to meet you."

Meredith lifted her hands, and Adnan reached over quickly to relieve her of the smaller bag so that she and Enes could shake hands. "It's nice to meet you, too."

A woman appeared behind Enes then, Poppy tucked into her arms. "Hi Meredith, I'm Celia. Adnan has told us a lot about you, and I'm so sorry that we had to cut your date short." She held up Poppy, who looked simultaneously pleased with herself and indignant at the way Celia was cradling her like a baby. "Actually, you're the one who should be sorry, Poppy. Pulling a daredevil stunt like that." She shook her head and then held the cat out to Adnan.

Adnan accepted the cat with one arm, holding out the bag for Celia with the other. "Thank you both so much. We brought you a little something for your trouble." He turned to Meredith with a smile. "Shall we get this little troublemaker home now? And get out of Enes and Celia's hair so they can enjoy a meal without too much begging?"

As if on cue, another cat appeared in the hallway, announcing herself with a loud meow. "Badem, good evening!" Adnan crouched down with Poppy in his arms as he greeted the cat. "My apologies for the interruption to your evening plans, ma'am." He held up Poppy who meowed quietly in protest. "I'll get this little one out of your hair now. I hope she didn't give you too much trouble."

Meredith was still taking it all in, the familiarity between Adnan and his neighbors, the apparent obsession all of these people had with their cats, and the cozy homey feeling of it all when Celia pulled her in for a quick hug.

"He really did talk about you a lot," Celia said quietly. "Just...you know. If he's playing it cool or anything like that, I just want it to be abundantly clear to you that that man is anything but cool when it comes to you."

Meredith schooled her expression into something resembling nonchalance, and when Celia released her from her embrace, the other woman's face did nothing to convey the secret they had just shared.

They exchanged a few more wishes for good evenings and good meals, though the goodbyes didn't last long with a squirming Poppy in Adnan's arms. As Enes and Celia retreated back to their apartment, Adnan smoothly unlocked the door to his home.

Inside, he didn't put Poppy back down on the floor despite her clear desire for him to do just that. Instead, he walked to the open balcony door, clucking at her all the way.

"The scene of the crime, eh?" He slid the door shut and locked it. "That'll keep you inside and out of the neighbors' apartment." Only then did he place the cat carefully on the ground. She immediately began to groom herself, as if she needed to wash off the contamination of being handled by humans, first by Celia and then by Adnan.

Adnan gestured around them then, before reaching up to rub the back of his neck. "This is...er, well, this is my home. Welcome!"

Meredith smiled, nodding as she set their dinner on the kitchen table. "It's lovely. I mean, what I've seen of it so far seems really...homey."

And it did. The kitchen opened into a living room, complete with a large green couch and matching armchair, a blanket that looked handknit draped across the back. There was art hanging on the walls and a bookshelf next to the TV full of battered paperbacks.

"Your neighbors seem really nice, too," she said. "I didn't really know what to expect when you said someone texted about a cat getting into her apartment."

He cocked his head at her. "How do you mean?"

"I mean...they could have been angry about it, you know? There could have been shouting and unpleasantness and your whole living environment could have felt really awkward as a result. But meeting them..." She exhaled a soft laugh. "Well, now that I've met them, seen how kind they were, I'm pretty sure they wouldn't have minded at all if we had stayed at the restaurant and finished our dinner." She held up her hands. "Not that I'm saying we should have done that. I'm glad we're here, glad we're about to dive into some delicious food right here in your nice cozy home. With Poppy." She smiled at the animal, who seemed to be nearly finished with her bath. "Oh! And that was really nice of you to bring some food for them. What was that you ordered? And when did you do it? I would have suggested it if I'd realized—"

He interrupted her with a gentle hand placed on her shoulder. "It's okay, Meredith. Everything is taken care of, and there's nothing you need to worry about." He nodded towards their forgotten meal, waiting for them on the table. "I just brought back a desert for them, but I got the same one for us, too. I hope you'll like it all. Shall we eat?"

"We shall." She rubbed her hands—*why were her palms getting sweaty?*—on the front of her pants and looked around. "What can I do to help? Point me in the direction of some way to make myself useful."

Adnan nodded in the direction of what appeared to be a cookie jar on the counter. "You can give Poppy a treat, so she will leave us alone when we're eating." He held up a hand in protest, but Meredith hadn't said a word and wasn't aware of even the vaguest glimmer of expression crossing her face. "I know what you're thinking. Does this man feed his cat from the table? If not, why would she beg? And I can assure you that Ms. Poppy does not eat any human food and is on a strict diet of only the best wet and dry cat food and I won't bore you with the details of all that." He took a breath. "But it is entirely possible that, in an effort to show off for you, our guest, a bit of mischief could happen. Especially given that there has already been more mischief on her part tonight than is typical. Anyway, I'm rambling, aren't I?" When she nodded, he gestured again towards the cookie jar. "There are some of those tube treats in there, and if you give one to Poppy, she'll love you forever."

Meredith smiled at him, warmed by the nerves he was so obviously feeling. If she had suddenly become aware of the fact that they were alone—cats didn't count—in his apartment, at least that understanding was having a similar effect on Adnan. Of course, his nerves could be about the fact that he hadn't cleaned for company or something equally innocuous, but judging by the state of the place, he had nothing to worry about. Sure, there were a few empty cardboard boxes here and there, but Meredith knew enough about cats to know that was all part of the package deal when you adopted one.

She opened the cookie jar, and as soon as she did, she felt a light pressure behind her knee. Glancing down, she saw that Poppy had materialized next to her and was standing with her two front paws pressing in at the top of her calf. She reached up with one paw, a more insistent meow escaping than Meredith had heard yet.

"Oh, you really like these, huh?" she asked, earning an enthusiastic response. Poppy even licked her lips and Meredith swore she saw the cat nod. She ripped the top off the tube and crouched down. If she had any doubt of how this paste treat thing worked, she was reassured to know that she was in the hands—*paws*—of an expert, as Poppy went right for the open end of the tube, licking fervently as Meredith squeezed up from the bottom like she was dispersing toothpaste.

The cat's little front paws were hugging Meredith's hand, as if she were helping her hold the tube, her little pink tongue and the intense focus in her eyes bringing a giggle out of Meredith's lips that she hadn't heard in years, if at all. When she glanced up, Adnan was watching them with a smile of his own fixed on his face.

Wow, he really loves his cat, she thought, aware that she was likely blushing as she gave him a small nod. Was she being ridiculous, too easily amused by something as normal as a cat eating a treat? She was so embarrassing...this was why she could never take herself anywhere, why it was, in general, a better idea to keep traveling and moving and exploring and not to spend too much time visiting someone's personal world.

But it was too late for that, for tonight at least. She got to her feet as Poppy's work on the tube was finished, leaving her new little friend to lick her lips and wash any remaining morsels of her treat off her whiskers. She held up the empty tube in Adnan's direction, raising her eyebrows as she asked him where the garbage was.

He was still looking at her like he knew a secret and wasn't sure if he should tell her, and she didn't like it one bit. Was he smiling at her? Was he so amused by her apparent cluelessness about all things cats? Had she done something wrong when she gave Poppy the treat? It wasn't her fault she'd never seen one of those tube things before. How was she supposed to know how it worked?

She threw away the packaging, then washed her hands. With her back to Adnan, she could swear she felt his eyes on her, the slight tingle at the base of her neck letting her know that he was watching her. But she dismissed it—did she want him to be watching her? Perhaps a part of her did. But she didn't want him watching her because he was amused by her cluelessness; she wanted him watching her because he was utterly enthralled by...well, by her.

Meredith gave the barest shake of her head as she turned around to face Adnan. There was no point in thinking such useless thoughts. No point in picking up an old crush simply because she was once again in the same place as the person her thoughts so often drifted back to. It wasn't, after all, as if her infatuation with Adnan was grounded in reality. How well could they possibly have known each other after spending just that one day together? No, if anything, it was simply an image of him that she had built up in her mind that was so compelling to her, and that made this real life, in-the-flesh version of him that much more dangerous.

Because, if she wasn't careful, she just might be tempted to believe that there was a spark between them. That Adnan was right and some mystical force had brought them together again. She knew better than that, though. For two people who built their careers around traveling, the world was a very small space. It was inevitable that their paths should cross again, and the fact that it had happened today didn't need to hold any special significance.

"Everything all right?" Adnan asked as she dried her hands on the towel. "I can pour a little more wine if you'd like that?"

Meredith shook her head. "Thanks, but no. I should keep a clear head. I mean, I've got a fairly packed itinerary in mind for tomorrow, and I don't want to be fuzzy for it."

He nodded. "A glass of water then."

When he had filled two glasses and taken a seat across from her at the table, they began to dig into the dishes arranged before them.

There were an assortment of chilled dishes, salads and yogurt-based meze, a wide variety of grilled meats, and a desert that looked like crispy shredded wheat covered with cream and green flakes. "What is this?" she asked, holding it up.

Adnan took it from her and placed it to the side. "That's künefe, our dessert. It's what I got for the neighbors, too. It's the best. It's got melted cheese inside and syrup and pistachios on the top. Don't look at me like that, you're going to love it!"

With the food to occupy them, Meredith relaxed. It wasn't that she wasn't comfortable with Adnan, but the comfort she felt with him brought a disconcerting feeling along with it. She was used to being on her own, was quite happy to explore the world with only her own company, trusting in her ability to keep herself happy and safe, no matter what obstacles might cross her path. The only other person she had felt like that with, particularly when traveling, was Adnan, on that one fateful day that they had shared.

"So," he began, dabbing at his mouth with a cloth napkin before speaking. "What is on this itinerary of yours for tomorrow? Where will you go? What will you do?" He chuckled once. "How early do you have to get up to fit in every item on the list?"

Meredith finished chewing as she considered the question. Even when he was teasing her, she couldn't be mad. She knew, after all, that the way she traveled suited her. She didn't need to convince him to see things her way, and she had no interest in throwing away her carefully crafted itineraries simply to suit his whims.

"It's a fairly packed day, I'll admit. But I'm up to it, especially since I'm not sharing a bottle of wine with you." She smiled to let him know she was teasing him back. "There's a bit more I'd like to see in Sultanahmet, since when you found me there yesterday, I was actually just doing a little pre-exploring exploring, if that makes sense."

"It...does not." He cocked his head at her. "So you weren't really there?"

"I was there." She exhaled something like a laugh through her nose. "I wasn't a mirage, and you really did see me. But I was just getting my bearings, just seeing what was in walking distance from the hotel. That's how I like to spend the first day, without too much planned since there is always the potential that particular day will be cut from the schedule due to travel delays and cancelations. When I manage to make it on time, I celebrate by walking around and taking it all in, and then the real work begins the next day."

"That sounds like another part of your itinerary that I may have influenced," said Adnan, tilting his head at an angle so that he was giving her a side eyed glance. "I thought there was only one afternoon built in for aimless wandering."

Meredith shook her head at him. "There's no need to get so excited about the ways you've impacted me as a traveler, Adnan. The free afternoon is all yours, and I give that credit where it is due. If I ever write a book about travel tips, I will cite you as the source of that particular gem."

"If you ever write a book about travel, I would prefer to have it be dedicated to me, rather than being named and shamed as a negative influence on your normally well-structured schedule."

She goggled at him. "Did you just casually ask me to dedicate a book to you?"

He nodded. "But the more important question before you get upset about that is…are you actually planning to write a book?"

Meredith sputtered. "That's not the point! You can't just ask for something like that. Now it's going to be hanging over my head, and if I ever do write a book, I'm going to feel guilty if I don't dedicate it to you."

"Again, I'll ask the question. Meredith, my dear, do you have any plans to write a book?"

She sighed. "No. No concrete plans, I mean. But I've thought about it. Who hasn't thought about writing a book?"

"Oh, I think a good many people out there love the thought of seeing their name in print on the cover of a book." Adnan nodded. "But a fraction of those people actually have the desire to write the dang thing, and that's where the disconnect happens." He gave her a warm smile then. "If you do decide to write a book, I release you from any obligation to dedicate it to me. You are free, little bird. Go. Fly away."

Meredith scoffed, shaking her head at him. "You are ridiculous. And just to be clear, the white space built into my itinerary on travel day is 100 percent not about you. It's about the deposits I didn't get back one too many times after my flights were delayed."

"Sure." He nodded at her and then had the audacity to wink. "Makes sense. And, by the way, while you no longer have any obligation to dedicate a hypothetical future book to me, I should warn you that Poppy will be absolutely crushed if you don't at least mention her."

At that, Meredith threw back her head and laughed, any lingering vestiges of anxiety evaporating into the night.

Ten

True to her plan, Meredith set out from the hotel bright and early the next morning. Adnan had insisted on driving her home the previous evening, and though she prided herself on being able to navigate just about any public transportation system on her own, she had accepted. It was nice to stay in his company just a bit longer, even as the mood of their time together shifted from light hearted and fun to a vague feeling of heaviness as she realized they were both about to disappear from each other's lives again.

The feeling hadn't lasted long, though. As Adnan pulled his car to a stop in front of the Begonvil, the question escaped before she had even unbuckled her seatbelt. "Would you mind some company tomorrow?" he asked, and if the night hadn't been so dark, she was almost sure she would have seen him blushing.

"You...want to come along on my rigid itinerary? Doesn't that go against everything you believe about traveling?"

He shrugged. "Maybe. But that isn't the point, is it? I want to spend more time with you." He darted a glance at her. "You can't be that surprised to hear me say it."

Couldn't she? It wasn't exactly the kind of thing people just came out and said, at least not in her experience of dating and men. But then again, Adnan did always do things a little differently, didn't he? Maybe he didn't even mean it *that* way, not anymore. Not after all the time that had passed and all the other people he had surely met in the interim. Had she even asked him if he had a girlfriend? She knew he didn't date much, but she hadn't actually confirmed that particular crucial fact. Wasn't that important information before they spent an entire day together?

It would also be important information before going out for a romantic dinner and the following him back to his place, no matter how innocent it all was, her brain reminded her.

"Er...you don't have a girlfriend, do you?" she blurted, grateful for the darkness as she felt her cheeks thrum with heat.

"Um." Adnan recoiled slightly, shaking his head. "No. No, I don't. No girlfriend, wife, partner, situationship, no one I'm 'talking to' or whatever the kids are saying these days." He had raised his hands to make air quotes in the middle of his sentence, and that got a soft chuckle out of Meredith.

"Good. I mean, I realized I should have asked that earlier, if there was someone whose feelings were going to be hurt by us going out for dinner or who would get the wrong idea if we spent the whole day playing tourist in the city where you live."

His eyes widened. "So that's a yes? I can tag along with you tomorrow?"

"Of course you can." She shook her head, just once. "It's your city, Adnan. You can do whatever you want in it."

"Right, but you know that's not what I'm asking. You *know* I don't just want to follow along six steps behind you to see how great this itinerary of yours is."

Meredith crossed her arms over her chest. "You could, though. If you wanted to get some new ideas for tours or whatever. It wouldn't bother me."

He reached over, gently pulling on her wrist until she released her closed-off position. "I want to spend the time with you. That's it. That's what it's about, and it's important to me that you don't misunderstand me. I missed you. I thought you were out of my life forever. And now you're here, and there is zero chance I'm going to let you be in the same city as me and not at least *try* to spend every possible moment I can with you. Okay?"

Meredith nodded, unable to find the words to respond to him.

"Wonderful. Then I'll meet you here at…let's see. Is seven early enough?"

Nodding again, she reached for the handle of the car door.

"Good night, Meredith. I'll see you in the morning."

Eleven

♥♥
♥

And that was how Meredith found herself exiting the hotel just before seven the next morning, feeling far less rested than she was normally accustomed to, running on butterflies and anticipation. As soon as the doors opened, her eyes found him, waiting with a grin on his face and two large cups in his hands.

It wasn't as if their eyes met across a crowded room, either. Despite being one of the largest cities in the world, the little corner of Istanbul that she could see and hear felt like it was still asleep, missing the hustle and bustle of so many other cities. Of course, there were groups of tourists assembling already, no doubt all having seen the same "best-kept secrets" tip suggesting that if they got to the Blue Mosque or the Hagia Sophia early enough, they could beat the crowds and snap the best pictures without having them all full of random strangers.

Adnan stepped forward to greet her and hand her a cup—coffee, judging by the smell of it. "Good morning." He smiled, raised his cup—a movement which she automatically mimicked—and then leaned in to brush his cheek against hers, the barest hint of his lips grazing over her skin.

Meredith recoiled slightly at the gesture, not in shock or disgust, but in surprise. She was startled by the intimacy but also by how easy, how natural it had felt to let herself be drawn towards Adnan as if by a magnetic force. She had only barely managed to stop herself from throwing her arms around his neck, though the hot beverage in her hand had been a perfect reality check. *What is going on with me? This wasn't like me at all.*

"Thank you for the...coffee?" She held up the beverage to him, and when he nodded, she took a sip. The coffee was strong, with just the right balance of bitterness and creamy warmth. "You remembered I like a lot of milk in my coffee?" she asked. "I'm impressed."

Adnan nodded, tipping his head to the side to indicate the sidewalk, which they began to follow together, walking at a leisurely pace in the direction of Sultanahmet's main attractions. "I did remember, but it wasn't hard to do. I started drinking my coffee the same way after tasting yours at that cafe in Prague."

"You did?" She turned to gape at him. "But you teased me about it so much! You said, if I remember correctly, that 'if you put that much milk and sugar in your coffee, what's the point of even drinking it?'"

Adnan grimaced. "Surely that's not what my voice sounds like?"

She let her jaw drop as she glared at him. "Not the point. But also, there was no sugar. Just a massive exaggeration on your part." She took another sip of her coffee. "It is satisfying, though, to know that I was right about the Great

Coffee Debate. Would have been nice if you had admitted to it at the time, but..." She shrugged. "Victory still tastes sweet, even eight years later."

"I wasn't holding out on you." He smiled at her as they began walking again. "I couldn't admit it even to myself at the time that you were right. It took a little more time—and drinking a few cups of milky coffee in the privacy of my own home—before I could admit that it was the superior way of drinking it." He shot a sly glance at her. "Just don't start about that whole 'putting milk in your tea' thing again." He shuddered. "I don't care how many millions of people in the world drink their tea that way—"

"Billions, probably," she interrupted.

He glared at her. "Doesn't matter. Turkish tea and milk don't go together, and that's the law."

"Fair enough." She was grinning unabashedly now. "Where did you get the coffee, anyway?" She studied the cup. "It doesn't look like it's from a big chain, not that I saw a Dunkin' Donuts anywhere around here."

"There's a little cafe near my apartment," said Adnan, taking a sip of his own coffee. "It's a cat cafe, actually, which...I mean, it isn't unusual to have a cat in a cafe in Turkey. It is unusual to make that a unique thing. Like, a formal arrangement between you as the owner and the cats as the...employees, I guess? But they make great coffee and the owner is nice." He glanced at Meredith then. "You might like it, actually. It's run by an American, and you would probably get along with her. I don't know if it's the kind of place you would write about in your articles, but surely you don't have to run every potential place you go by whether you would write about it."

Meredith pulled a face, sticking her tongue out at him. "I'll have you know that I can actually go anywhere I want and do anything I want to do. A perk of working for myself, I suppose. And I do have that free afternoon, so why not stop by this cafe of yours? I'm not the biggest cat lover, but that doesn't mean I couldn't appreciate a cute little cafe with some furry friends."

"Ooh, wait until I tell Poppy what you said about not being a cat lover." Adnan was shaking his head. "You are going to hear about it from her next time you see her."

The mention of Poppy came with a pang that surprised Meredith. "Okay, she might be the exception to that rule." She glanced around. "You didn't bring her with you today?"

Adnan turned out his pockets. "I did not. I offered, but the itinerary was a little too intense for her. Not to worry, she's the furthest thing from bored at home without me."

She raised an eyebrow at him. "You didn't leave the balcony open again, did you?"

"I didn't. But she and Badem had such a nice time playing together yesterday that I gave Enes and Celia the key to my apartment and they're going to bring her over later for a play date."

"Wow. I've never heard of cats having play dates before. Dogs and kids, sure, but cats?"

Adnan smiled, looping an arm through hers. "Stick with me, honey, and I'll teach you about all the adorable and surprising things cats do."

Twelve

♥♥

They had walked so many steps that even Meredith was tired, and this was all in a day's work for her. But the two explorers had returned to the Blue Mosque, ventured over to the Hagia Sophia, visited Topkapı Palace, and checked out all the vendors in the Grand Bazaar before heading across the bridge to Galata Tower.

By early afternoon, Meredith was tired—ready to sit someplace comfortable, drink something caffeinated, and jot down a few notes about what they had seen so far. When she mentioned that to Adnan, he nodded and then guided her to a cafe with a nice view of the tower.

They ordered drinks—and desserts, at Adnan's insistence—and took their purchases upstairs and out onto a balcony. The view of the city was stunning, prompting Meredith to snap a few pictures of the view across the water before sitting down to enjoy her cappuccino and the assortment of baklava they had gotten to share.

"Thank you for coming with me today," she said as she licked a stray chopped pistachio from her finger. "This all wouldn't have been nearly as enjoyable without you."

Adnan smiled, taking a sip of his tea. "Believe it or not, I'm enjoying my own city even more, just getting to experience it with you. We should do this more often." His last words tumbled out of him, quicker and quieter than the words before them. "I mean, at least more than every eight years."

"Oh definitely," said Meredith, playing it cool. Adnan seemed so nervous about what he had said, perhaps because he was afraid she would misinterpret it. Well, she could help him out there. "I can let you know about any trips I have planned and if you happen to have the time and the miles, you would always be welcome to join."

But he only shook his head. "Not that that doesn't sound great, but it isn't really good enough, is it? I mean, would you be satisfied with that? With...what, spending a day or two together every six months?"

It would be a hell of a lot less lonely that what I'm doing right now, she thought, barely beginning to nod. "Well, it does seem like the logical next step, doesn't it? Surely you aren't suggesting...what, moving in together?" She forced out a laugh. "I know we get along well, Adnan, but two days spent together in eight years is not the backbone for a long-term commitment."

"It's not...I wasn't..." Adnan was flustered. "I'm not proposing marriage or anything like that. I'm just thinking...I don't know, doing this while you're here in Istanbul, not just today, but for the rest of your trip might be fun. And then maybe...I don't know if you've considered exploring more of Turkey, but Poppy and I are very up for that."

Now there was an idea she hadn't considered. "I would *love* to see more of Turkey. It's like...I can already tell from these few days that I won't be done after this trip is over."

"Good then." He nodded. "Do you already have a plan in place, for where you're going next, I mean?"

Meredith shook her head. "I actually don't. I was planning to figure that out at some point, I guess, thinking that there might be some act of serendipity that would make the next steps clear. Like an email from an editor suggesting they would love to share a piece about Santo Domingo or travel trends in cruise ships." She shrugged, letting the words tumble out before she had even admitted them to herself. "So far, the next step hasn't revealed itself and I was actually thinking that extending my stay here and taking an actual vacation might be just what I need to feel refreshed and recharged."

Adnan's grin was wide. "Really? That's amazing. It would be wonderful to have you around a bit longer, and I hadn't even considered that your trip might be open-ended." He rubbed his hands together like a cartoon villain. "Oh, the trouble we could get into. Now that it seems like we have more time to work with, the ideas are flowing."

"Nothing illegal," she cut in. "I would, for example, love to sail on the Bosphorus, but I would *not*, however, appreciate going to jail for hijacking a boat to make that particular dream come true."

"Noted," said Adnan with a serious nod before flashing her a smile that would have made her go weak in the knees if she had been standing. "So you were waiting on serendipity, huh?"

Meredith nodded. "I guess so."

He shook his head. "And you thought it hadn't intervened?" He scoffed. "Have you ever seen something more serendipitous that this?" He gestured between them. "I hate to play two roles in your little fairy tale—is it even legal for one person to be both the leading man *and* the fairy godperson?—but I think the hand of fate knows *exactly* what it is doing here." He reached for his tea then, but she could see the broad grin hiding behind his cup as he sipped.

She didn't know what to say to that. Adnan's ease with joking about a love story blooming between them confused her. She wasn't naive enough to think he actually meant what he was saying, but she wished she had a larger sampling of experience with him to pull from to know what the man was really like. Sure, the evening before had been special, unlike anything she'd experienced in a long time. But could she trust that in the light of day?

Did he flirt with everyone? Was there some hapless fellow traveler who had followed him around with puppy eyes in every port, every city he had ever visited? Was she even remotely special to him, or was he just simply the sort of extroverted, flirtatious person who made everyone feel special and never let anyone really get to know him or claim him as their own?

And in that moment, as that thought landed, she'd had enough. *I'm 31 years old, and I am done playing games. I didn't like these games when I was a teenager, and I like them even less now.*

Meredith set down her tea glass, took a deep breath, and licked her lips. "Adnan," she said, waiting for him to look up.

"Yeah?" And then again, when he saw the expression on her face. "Yeah, Mer? What's up? Is something wrong?"

She shook her head. "Nothing is wrong, but...well, I'm sorry to ruin the fun, but I just have to ask. Are you flirting with me? And if you are, are you doing it because you flirt with everyone? I know we've *barely* spent any time together, and it's frankly absurd of me even to care about this but—"

"I'm flirting with you," he interrupted as he placed a hand on her fingers, which were tapping on the table, the first she had become aware of what they were doing. "And I want to be clear with you that, while I *am* unusually charming and friendly and just an absolute delight"—he looked into her eyes then and she saw something shift, a lightheartedness give way to something serious, a vow—"I am not treating you the same way I treat everyone else. I'm not just trying to show you a good time in Istanbul or have a little fun together for a few days." Adnan's hand tightened on hers. "I know it sounds cheesy, but I *do* believe in fate. Or at least in being given a second chance not to let something great slip away. I've thought about you more than I should considering how long we knew each other in Prague. I'm really glad you're here. And I'm not letting you get away again."

She raised an eyebrow at him.

Adnan winced. "It was going great until the end there, right? But I swear I didn't mean 'I'm not letting you get away again' in, like, the way a serial killer would mean it. Of course you are always free to go. Hell, I'll even drive you to the airport." He smiled at her. "I just meant I didn't want you to leave again without us at least having this conversation." He squeezed her hand then. "And I'm sorry if you felt unsure, felt like you had to ask if you were special to me. Because I should have made that abundantly clear to you from the first moment I saw you again. You are *very* special to me." He gestured between them. "There's nothing else like this in my world. No one else who could be sitting in that chair in your place."

Meredith's cheeks had started heating before he had even started speaking—*had she ever asked a more embarrassing question than the one that had initiated his monologue?*—and they hadn't stopped. Adnan's gaze was locked on hers, and the intensity in his eyes made her feel unequipped to deal with such large emotions, such tender proclamations, something that felt so much like it was the beginning of something.

She was good at being in a relationship, especially a long-distance one. She was good at having someone as a fixture in her life, or maybe in the outskirts of her life. Someone to check in with at the end of the day, to make plans to meet up with when it suited both of their schedules...but she had never merged her life with someone else's.

She had never wanted to.

And she had never much enjoyed the beginning of a relationship, the butterflies and uncertainties and lost sleep. No, Meredith was nothing if not practical, and that extended to her relationships as well.

But this...whatever was happening between her and Adnan, it was different. Sure, those same "early relationship" sensations were there, but this time? Well, this time, they weren't offensive.

She gulped. No, they weren't offensive. They were downright *scary*.

"I...uh..." She finally spoke up. "I appreciate the clarity." She nodded. "I really do. I like you, you like me, and well...uh, well now we both know that for sure." She forced a smile. "It's good, it really is."

Adnan frowned. "Then why do I feel like your face isn't matching with your words? Mer, that"—he pointed to her face—"is not the look of someone who is happy, feeling good and excited about a new relationship." He shook his head, just once. "Please don't force anything on my account. If you aren't interested, you aren't interested. We're friends, you know? We can stay friends. Nothing needs to change."

And even though his words were everything she *should* want to hear, Meredith shook her head. "No, it's not that. It's just that...well, to be honest, I don't know how any of this works."

"Any of what works?" He leaned in closer. "If you're asking me for dating lessons or kissing lessons or anything in that vein, I will be *very* agreeable to the idea of being your exclusive instructor."

Meredith laughed despite the seriousness of the emotions warring inside her. "I'm very glad to know that, but that's not what I meant. I just mean..." She trailed off as she sighed, finding the words. "You live here. You have a cat. I travel for a living. I like my life, and from the looks of it you like yours, too. So...*that*. That is what I'm having a hard time understanding. How we are supposed to make this work."

Adnan's face spread in a broad smile. "Oh, *that*. I thought it was something serious." He reached for her hand across the table. "I'm afraid to say it, but I think you're getting ahead of yourself, my dear. For right now, for today, is it enough to simply know that I have feelings for you and you, from the sound if it, also have feelings for me?" His grip on her hand tightened. "Wait a second. I bared my soul to you, and I'm just now realizing that I'm only sort of connecting the dots to infer that you reciprocate my feelings. Do you, in fact....er, *like* me? I mean, are we on the same page about all of this?"

Meredith nodded as she squeezed his hand back. "We are very much on the same page, Adnan. Would I be worrying about how to make our futures compatible with each other if I didn't...er, *like* you?"

"Interesting," he said. "You sort of skipped right over the happy, exciting part, the part where no one is in unrequited love with the other and you focused right in on potential problems and roadblocks." There was a twinkle in his eye, his gaze fixed tightly on hers. "Would you be open to just enjoying this first part with me, before we spend too much time and energy figuring out how it's all going to work out in the end?"

Meredith sighed. She wanted to throw her cares away, to agree with him that it *would* be much nicer to enjoy today without worrying about tomorrow. The only problem...

"It's a romantic idea, Adnan. It really is. The only problem is, frankly, that I'm so good at preparing for future contingencies that an outside observer might mistake me for being psychic."

Adnan nearly did a spit take with the last sip of his tea. "I'm sorry? How is you being psychic a problem?"

"I'm not psychic. It's just that my mind is always juggling any number of itineraries and adjustments and alternatives and after years of living that way, I don't know if I possess the ability to just sit back and enjoy something without thinking about its future implications." She forced a smile. "It's not that I don't want to enjoy being here, being with you. Of course I do. But are we really going to throw caution to the wind and begin something when we don't even know if we're on the same page? Isn't that, like, a core rule of dating once you're no longer a teenager?" She gestured wildly. "You hear those stories all the time...the couple dates for years but it's only seven years down the road that they realize one of them wants kids and the other one doesn't." She shook her head. "Everyone always says they should have talked about it sooner, but..." She let her words trail off as she sighed.

"Hey." Adnan came around the table, edging in next to her on the booth side. "Hey. Look at me."

Meredith shook her head, refusing to meet his eyes. "I just heard what I said, and I know I'm being ridiculous. I mean, I'm not asking you if you want kids—"

"I'm undecided," he said. "Please. Look at me." When she did, he reached up and cupped her chin. "Here's what I know. I've seen those stories too, about the couples who had some sort of dealbreaker that they never revealed to each other, and when it finally came out, it was too late. And I understand how that's scary."

Meredith nodded. "It is. And it makes it sort of impossible to just be a *fun times, go with the flow* kind of gal, you know?"

"I do. I mean, a *fun times, go with the flow* kind of guy in my case, but yeah. But here's the thing for me: I only have one dealbreaker, and I'll lay it out for you right now."

"Only one?"

He nodded. "Poppy and I are a package deal. You take me, you take her, too." There wasn't a hint of a joke in his eyes. "Can you agree to that?"

"Of course. I would never give you some kind of 'me or Poppy' ultimatum."

"Good, then." His smile had returned. "And what about you? What are your dealbreakers?"

Meredith shook her head. "It isn't that simple. What about...everything else? Like...do you want to live in Istanbul? Do you see yourself getting married? Do you want kids?"

"All things I am open to figuring out," he said. "There is nothing in life I am as attached to as Poppy. I am, after all, responsible for her well-being. And I love my family, I love my country...but I am not looking for someone who will fit into my life as it already is. I am looking for someone to make a new life with. That's what we're talking about." His foot nudged hers under the table. "So go on, then. What about you? Don't be shy."

"I..." A wave of embarrassment washed over Meredith. After that whole speech of hers, she was only now realizing she didn't have nearly the level of clarity that Adnan did. "I haven't thought about it. Not like you have." She pushed her empty glass to the center of the table. "I like my life the way it is, I guess."

"Who wouldn't? It's a great life." He gave her an encouraging smile. "So does that mean you'd like to keep things the way they are now? Freelance travel writing? No home base?"

"I mean..." Her cheeks were heating again. *Why was it so hard to express what was important to her?* "I do want to keep traveling," she said. "I have no desire to move somewhere, put down roots and never leave."

"Makes sense. Is there a certain percentage of time you want to spend traveling? I'm guessing right now you're at about 90 percent, since if I'm remembering correctly you generally spend about a month each year back with your family."

"That's right," she said. "And no, it doesn't have to be that much. I hadn't really thought of it in terms of percentage before." She sighed. "But when you put it that way, 90 percent is a lot. And I might like to reduce that a little."

"Great." Adnan was grinning now. "So it sounds to me like that's something that's up for discussion, not a deal-breaker unless the option becomes no travel at all, which seems highly unlikely for either one of us." He steepled his hands under his chin. "What else? Kids? Marriage? Eight cats and twelve dogs? A preference of where you live?"

She shrugged. "I don't know about those things, either. I think I've assumed for so long that I would just be on my own that...I don't know, I figured they were off the table."

"Do you want them to stay off the table?"

She shook her head. "I don't know. I think I want to figure it out together."

"And if you get clarity, if you have a sudden strong feeling that you know what you want, that you figured it out...will you tell me?"

Her reply came immediately. "Of course. And you'll do the same?"

Adnan nodded. "Of course."

Meredith exhaled a long sigh. "Then that's not so scary after all, now is it?"

"Nothing seems scary about the future when I imagine figuring it out with you. Not even...I don't know, traffic patterns when we're all driving flying cars!"

Meredith laughed then, relief at arriving at the other side of a conversation she had dreading flooding through her veins. She reached for Adnan then, pulling him closer as he wrapped his arms around her and she relaxed into the embrace.

Thirteen

In the days that followed, Meredith and Adnan approached their budding relationship with something like kid gloves. Neither one of them wanted to dive in too deep too quickly and risk scaring away the potential before it had the time to truly blossom. They spent their days exploring the city together, and in the evenings, Meredith returned to her hotel room to write and check in with herself.

There was a part of her that wondered what it would be like to truly follow her heart, to let herself be inseparable from Adnan. He had made it clear that she was welcome to stay over at his apartment any time she wanted, but she had held firm in her assertion that she needed time, needed space, needed to handle all of this like it was delicate.

Because it was.

Meredith knew enough about self sabotage to know that if things changed too quickly in her world, her ego was likely to sound the warning bell to alert her to the fact that she was leaving familiar—and therefore "safe"—territory in favor of the Unknown. It would only be a matter of time, then, before she would blow things up with Adnan, either by picking a fight over the most inane of disagreements or by acting impulsively, booking a one-way flight to Vietnam and only letting him know when she was already on the plane.

And so they treaded carefully. She extended her stay at the hotel for another week, and continued to stay there even though there were together every day. There was no more talk about the future, no use of words like "love" or "commitment." It was almost possible, then, for Meredith to forget that the conversation at the cafe in Galata had happened, so seamlessly had they slipped back into their roles as friends. Or, rather, as friends who clearly liked each other, because the flirtation was far from absent.

On that particular evening, Meredith had agreed to accompany Adnan to Kedi Cafe, the cat cafe in his neighborhood.

"Will Poppy be joining us then?" she asked, surprised by how much she had missed the little creature, who hadn't joined one of their adventures since the night she had Houdini-ed her way out of the apartment. As much as Adnan might deny it, it seemed he truly had grounded the little girl in retribution.

He shook his head. "It's not that kind of cafe. I mean, it's for humans and there are cats there. But they don't generally serve cats. Like, it's not a cafe that cats go to and pay for their kibble with dead mice or anything like that."

"No, I figured that much," said Meredith with a smile and a shake of her head. "Believe it or not, I am familiar with the concept of a cat cafe and also aware that cats don't have pockets or money to put in them." She paused for a moment, her brow wrinkling as she considered Adnan's statement. "Also, who ever heard of a restaurant where you trade food for different food?"

"Sorry?"

The confusion on his face mirrored her own, and she laughed. "You said something about cats trading dead mice for kibble and, I mean, I've never eaten a mouse, but I can't imagine trading a juicy steak for a bowl of cereal."

"An excellent point. I realize now I need to be a lot more careful about my metaphors, considering who I am speaking with."

"Believe it or not, I generally don't write about rodents—or even cats, for that matter—in my travel articles."

"No? Well, good luck writing about Istanbul without mentioning cats. They are one of the more noteworthy features of the city."

Meredith nodded. "Oh, I know. I've been here long enough to notice the presence of cats, well, everywhere." She held up her hands before he could protest. "I'm not complaining. I think, actually, I've had a bit of a change of heart where it comes to the little guys."

Adnan shot a glance at her. "It's against my belief system to acknowledge any way of feeling about cats that isn't 100 percent approval." He sniffed. "Still, I'm glad you're coming around. But maybe you should wait to crow about how much you love cats until after we've gone to the cafe. Just in case you feel differently afterwards."

"Okay, then. And maybe, if I'm not all catted out, we could stop by your place afterwards to say hello to Poppy? I do actually miss her."

"You do?"

"Definitely. Why? Do you think she missed me, too?"

Adnan smiled. "I think you'll just have to wait and see about that. You can ask her yourself."

Fourteen

Kedi Cafe was everything Meredith never knew she needed in a cafe. Awash with sunlight, cozily warm, and full of peacefully sleeping cats, it instantly felt more like home than any hotel had ever. The woman behind the counter greeted them with a broad smile, hurrying out from behind the register to give Adnan a quick hug and then pull Meredith into an embrace.

"It's so nice to meet you," she said, pulling back to grin at Meredith. "Celia told me all about you, and I stalked you online and read a bunch of your articles. I'm Jasmine." She held out a hand for Meredith to shake and then continued. "I especially loved the piece about Tokyo. It almost made me want to travel there!" She gestured to the cafe around them. "Though, as you can probably imagine, it's a little tricky to just pack up and leave when I need to run this place. My grandmother, though, is currently living her dream life on a cruise ship, and I sent her a few of your articles, the ones about Grenada and St. Lucia."

"Oh, great." Meredith nodded, struggling to find the words to respond to this woman's enthusiasm. She looked around at the cafe, noticing two cats batting around a crumpled receipt. "This is a lovely place you have here. Can't say I've ever seen anything quite like it."

Jasmine's face split in a broad smile. "Thank you so much. I adore it, of course. It was my grandmother's cafe originally, a little passion project to keep her busy during her retirement. That is, of course, until she swindled me into 'running it while she went on a little vacation.'" Jasmine had raised her fingers to make air quotes. "I'm not complaining, though. You know how it is, I'm sure, when you fall in love with a place, a cat, and a guy and end up changing all of your plans because of it."

Meredith felt herself recoil at Jasmine's words almost automatically. "Is that what happened to you? All of it, I mean?"

Jasmine nodded. "Sure is. It's hard to say which one I fell in love with first, since it all happened at the same time. I started running the cafe, adopted a mischievous kitten, and then of course there is Burak."

Meredith raised an eyebrow. "And Burak is...?"

"Burak is the fortunate man who has Jasmine as his other half." It was time for Adnan to chime in. "And I suppose the right question is really *where* is Burak?" He looked around them as if Burak might be hiding under one of the tables.

"He's actually at work, believe it or not," said Jasmine. "Not all of us are so fortunate as to work in cat cafes, though he does conduct a fair amount of his business from that table over there." She nodded towards a table in the corner where one small orange cat was sleeping. "Cheddar knows it too. Looks like he's waiting for Burak to show up for a meeting or something."

Meredith was silent as she turned slowly in place, taking in her surroundings. She wasn't sure what she had expected from a cat cafe—she knew the novelty of such a place wasn't restricted to Istanbul, and yet she had never managed to visit the cat cafes in any other city where she had traveled. She had expected some level of chaos, undoubtedly, perhaps grouping cat cafes in with goat yoga and puppy painting classes in her mind. And yet what rose to the top as she surveyed Kedi Cafe was peace, comfort, and no shortage of sleepy cats.

Right, she thought. *The chaotic energy comes from kittens. Older cats sleep for, like, 27 hours a day.* She chuckled under her breath. She may have expected only to visit the cafe out of some kind of obligation to accept Adnan's offer, but now that she was here?

Well, now that she was here, she couldn't imagine a better place in the whole city to park herself with her laptop and write for hours on end. And if she could spend those hours with a sleeping cat curled up next to her, then all the better.

"I love it here," she murmured to Adnan, prompting him to lean in closer. "I want to make it my informal office. Write here four days a week. Have a regular order and a table with my name on it."

Adnan grinned at her. "I had a feeling you would."

She frowned. "How could you possibly have known that? Until today, I had done nothing to suggest I was destined to be a cat lady."

"Not a *cat lady*!" Jasmine interjected. "As if such a thing exists. There are only cat ladies and people who don't know they are cat ladies yet." She cleared her throat. "I should clarify that in this context, *lady* is not a gender-specific word. Burak is a cat lady, and he knows it. Adnan, you are too."

"Oh, of course." Adnan was nodding. "I could never deny that. Poppy would have my head." He turned back to Meredith. "I suppose you'll just have to consider that I know you better than you might expect." He leaned closer, lowering his voice conspiratorially. "And you haven't even tried their carrot cake yet." Turning back to Jasmine, he chewed his lower lip. "Could we get two, please? And a couple of coffees as well?"

"Coming right up," said Jasmine with a nod. "Pick any table and make yourselves at home." She reached out and squeezed Meredith's upper arm. "And I really do mean that. I'd be so happy to have you here as a regular customer. And I'm not even saying that because I'm secretly hoping you'll write up the cafe in your Istanbul piece. Imagine that!"

They found seats by the window and were immediately greeted by a tuxedo cat who sniffed the air, meowed loudly, and then jumped right up onto Meredith's lap. She laughed as she pet the cat's head, his purrs immediately beginning and then cranking up in volume until she felt like she might have to yell to be heard over them.

"You have a great life here," she told Adnan as she scratched behind the cat's ears. "Every place you show me, every acquaintance of yours that you introduce me to who treats me like they're genuinely happy to meet me..." She shook her head once. "I can't lie. It all adds up to making a very powerful case for spending more time in Istanbul than originally planned."

"Then my plan has been a success." Adnan pumped his fist. "Sorry, I don't know why I did that," he said with a self-deprecating laugh. "That's not a gesture that's in my usual repertoire. I am glad, though, that Istanbul is making such a good impression on you. So you don't feel like you've already seen all there is to see? Like it's time to move on?"

Meredith shook her head. "Not at all. You know I was never much for the kind of travel where you try to fit 17 cities into a 12-day tour."

"No, I remember that. That's why we connected in Prague, after all."

She frowned. "What do you mean?"

"You don't remember?" he asked. When she shook her head, he continued. "We were the only ones left. Everyone else who was there at the same time as us had already moved on after two days—more than enough time to see the Prague Castle and the Charles Bridge, and what else was there that the city had to offer, anyway, as far as they were concerned? When I realized you were the only one who wasn't checking out the next day, that's when I approached you."

"No." Meredith was still shaking her head, more firmly now. "We only met each other that day that we spent together, didn't we? We bumped into each other outside the hostel, realized we were going in the same direction, and that was history. We didn't meet before that, I'm sure of it."

"Maybe we didn't meet, but that didn't mean I didn't notice you." He gave her a playful frown. "You mean to tell me that you didn't notice me?"

She sighed. *Why did it feel so vulnerable to admit this, even when he had already revealed his full hand of cards?* "Okay. Maybe I noticed you. In that, I was vaguely aware of you in the same way that I was vaguely aware of everyone else in the hostel." Noticing his confused expression, she continued. "I mean that when you're a woman traveling alone, it's a good idea to size up all the guys. You know, make mental notes of who seems harmless and who you definitely don't want to bump into in a dark corner. On second thought, though, seeming harmless isn't exactly a rock solid criteria for judging the character of a stranger. If true crime documentaries have taught us anything, it is that."

"Right." He pursed his lips. "So you were aware of me and had apparently decided that I was not a threat?"

Meredith nodded. "That's right. Not that any of the others were, either. None of them had any travel companion potential though, either, so that's why I pretty much kept to myself. When you and I were left alone, that's when I decided to take a chance on you."

"You mean it wasn't dumb luck that brought us together that day? You're what...some kind of mastermind?"

She scoffed softly as she crossed her arms over her chest. "You mean you really believed my little stunt with the map? That I couldn't figure out how to get to the Kafka Museum from the hostel? Please! I've been reading maps since before I *could* read, Adnan. I could easily have found my way there, but I wanted to spend that day with you."

Adnan nodded back at her, but his serious expression was ruined by the grin spreading across his face. "That changes everything, Meredith."

"How so?"

"Simple," he said, leaning forward to lift her hand and press his lips to the backs of her knuckles. "Now I know all your secrets. And there's no use pretending any of this is casual at all when we both know we've wanted it to be more for a very long time."

And there was, simply, nothing she could say in response to that. There was no point in denying what was so obviously true, no benefit at all to holding onto the pretense that this thing that was sprouting deep roots connecting her to Adnan was something casual, something she could walk away from without a single regret. She had let herself imagine for so long what it would be like if things had been different between them, and now that they were, there was nothing to do but thank her lucky stars and let herself fall.

Fifteen

After that fateful day at Kedi Cafe, Meredith let herself relax into her changed relationship with Adnan. Or perhaps, she *made* herself relax into it, since after years of being on her own, accountable only to herself and to her own whims, the idea of relaxing, of practicing giving and taking with a partner, was as foreign to her as any arrivals gate ever had been.

But she didn't relax all the way. No, as much as Adnan insisted that she was more than welcome to stay in his apartment, that there was even a second bedroom where they could set up a desk for her to complete her writing assignments, she couldn't stomach the idea of taking their relationship to that level.

"Just because I like you so much, that doesn't mean I think I should live with you," she told him, before standing on her toes to drop a soft kiss on his lips. "In fact, it's *because* I like you so much that I'm pretty sure moving in together would be a bad idea."

"That's fair," he said, biting his lips to camouflage his badly hidden pout. "But if our relationship is in danger of ending because staying in that hotel is getting too expensive, let's find an alternate plan, okay?"

"Of course," she said, her pulse picking up with the news she had to share with him. "I didn't tell you yet, but I reached an agreement with *Voyager*, and they're going to publish my whole Istanbul series." She shook her head, feeling positively gleeful at what was in store for her, for them. "It's going to be a series of six articles, one published per week, focusing on different aspects of the city. Because, after all, who could fit all of Istanbul into one measly travel article?"

"Thatta girl," said Adnan, pulling her in for an embrace. "Or woman, rather. I'm proud of you, Mer. And beyond relieved that you have already figured out a way to keep yourself in Istanbul longer than originally planned. Have you given any thought to what comes after all those pieces are published?"

Meredith shook her head. "I'd like to stick around longer, live on my savings for a bit while I figure out the next step. Actually, ever since we joked about it the other day, I've been thinking about writing a book, and this could be a great time to do it. I mean, I've done nothing but save money for years and years, and if I can't give myself a bit of a buffer to try my hand at something new, then what *is* the point of making that money in the first place?"

"An excellent question." Adnan looked lost in thought as they fell back into step on their nightly walk to yet another up and coming restaurant. "Do you want me to keep my eyes and ears open for a possible place for you to stay? I might have an idea…" He trailed off then. "Never mind that," he said with a dismissive wave of his hand. "Let's talk about literally anything else but the future. How about the present? Reading any good books lately?"

She peered at him, narrowing her eyes but resisting the urge to insist he tell her about whatever plan he was cooking up in his head. "I browsed through the English section of a bookstore yesterday, picked up some Orhan Pamuk and Elif Shafak."

Adnan nodded. "Do you do that everywhere, read local authors?"

"I mean, I try to. It isn't always practical to pick up physical books though, and sometimes I don't stay long enough to read as much as I'd like. My e-reader is full of books I'm intending to read one day when I have the time." She scoffed. "I think every book lover says that, though. But for as long as I'm hoping to be here, it only made sense to get a few paperbacks, start building a collection."

"So you're telling me you're going to need a place with a bookshelf, the way things are going. I'll add that to my list of requirements for your accommodation." He smiled at her then, patting her just once on the shoulder. "But don't worry. I'll build you one if it doesn't come with your apartment."

"Oh, are you a carpenter in addition to being a tour guide? Is there a workshop full of tools somewhere I should know about?" she teased.

Adnan just shook his head. "Believe it or not, no. I didn't mean, like, I would chop down a tree in the park, mill the logs, and make you a custom bookcase from scratch. It was more...well, we can go to Ikea or the supermarket or the mall and find a big enough bookshelf there. One where you only need a hammer or a screwdriver to put it together. Or one of those handy little Allen wrenches that only fits that exact piece of furniture. I probably have a drawer full of them after all the end tables and desks I've put together over the years."

"Well, that does sound like a nice project." Meredith smiled up at him as they walked on, aware but unsurprised by just how relaxed she felt despite the uncertainty about where she would be staying next. She knew Adnan was there, looking out for her, and she knew that no matter what happened, it would all be part of the new adventure of her life.

Sixteen

"I have to show you something," said Adnan the following evening when he opened the door of his apartment to greet her.

"And hello to you too," she responded. "Don't you want to ask me how my day was or...I don't know, give me a hug before we do show and tell?" She raised an eyebrow at him. "Is this, like...a *spicy* 'I have to show you something' or is it more of a three-year-old saying it, and you're going to show me that you have a snapping turtle in your bathtub and then beg me to let you keep him?"

He pulled her in for a hug then, dropping a quick kiss on the top of her head. "Would you believe it's actually neither of those things?"

Meredith gasped in mock horror. "You mean there's a secret third option that I hadn't even considered? My faith in my understanding of the universe is crumbling before my very eyes."

"Yes, yes. Well..." He gave her a gentle push backwards before following her out into the hallway and closing the door to his apartment behind him. "Let's get you to your surprise, then."

"It isn't even in your apartment?" She narrowed her eyes at him. "If you take me outside and show me a car with a giant bow on it, please know in advance that I have no interest in driving in Istanbul. Not now, not ever."

"Duly noted," said Adnan with a solemn nod. "The traffic in this city is a living nightmare, so no, I didn't buy you a car."

"Good." She nodded and began to follow him down the stairs. "And uh..." She hesitated over her next words, knowing she was about to make a joke about a delicate topic and yet still wishing to communicate her honest wishes. "Well, if you're about to propose to me, I do appreciate a romantic gesture, and at the same time, I think it is too soon for that."

He stopped in the middle of the flight of stairs and turned back to face her. "Not interested in being proposed to two weeks into a relationship?" He shook his head, but he was smiling. "Now I've heard everything."

Meredith let out a small sigh, and they continued to follow the stairs down to the floor below Adnan's apartment. As they approached one of the doors, he pulled out a key from his pocket and fit it into the lock.

"What are you doing?" she asked, though the answer was obvious.

"Just wait and see," he said, pushing the door open as the two of them stepped inside.

The apartment was the mirror image of Adnan's apartment, with the kitchen and living room in the exact opposite places they were upstairs. Meredith took it all in, nodding as he pointed out the small workspace in the living room, complete with two nice bookcases.

"It's lovely," she said, "and looks quite familiar, too. Like looking at your apartment in a mirror, except with slightly more feminine taste." She looked up at him in expectation. "Are you moving down here or...?"

Adnan shook his head and held the key out to her. "No, but you could if you want to." He gestured around them. "This is the apartment Celia was renting when she moved here. I guess the company she was working for at the time found it for her, but when she decided to stay on, she took over the lease herself. Of course, now that she and Enes are engaged, she has moved in with him upstairs."

"But she's still paying rent down here?"

Adnan nodded. "She is. Of course, if you wanted to sublease it from her, the rent would be very reasonable. It would work out in favor of both of you."

Meredith looked around the living room again with fresh eyes. "All of this space?"

Adnan nodded. "All of this space. A little more than any of the hotel rooms you've been living in lately, I guess?"

She laughed. "I don't know if I've had this much space since I lived with my parents. And this kitchen..." She was practically drooling over the fact that it had an oven *and* a dishwasher.

"So you like it?"

"Of course! And do you want to know what the best thing is?"

"Absolutely."

Meredith stepped towards him and wrapped her arms around his waist. "We would be neighbors. We could see each other every day. And we would have time to figure out...well, *us*. What the future holds." She pulled back slightly to look up at him. "Would you want that?"

He scoffed at her. "I'm the one showing you this apartment and highlighting all of its very best features and *still* you have to ask if I want you to live here?" He leaned down slightly and pressed a kiss on the tip of her nose. "The only thing better than having you here would be having you in my apartment, but even *I* know it's too soon to ask you to move in."

Meredith nodded. "Then I think I should take it."

"Really?" When she smiled and nodded a little more firmly, he kissed her again. "Because there was something I wanted to ask you, and now seems like a great time to do it."

"Oh yeah? What's that?" She grinned at him, already feeling like the space around her belonged to her somehow. "We already established that you aren't proposing and you aren't asking me to move in with you, so I'm curious what other big questions remain."

"How would you feel, after you finish writing your Istanbul pieces, of course, about taking a trip to the Mediterranean coast with me and Poppy? We could see the sights together, you could write about it, and I could plan an itinerary for leading tour groups there?"

"And Poppy? What would she do?"

"The same thing she does here. Enjoy the sights, eat the best cat food there is, and sleep for more hours than I can count. Basically, live the ultimate life of luxury."

She let her smile wash over her. "It sounds like a perfect plan, then."

"So that's a yes?"

"Absolutely. I have a feeling it's always going to be a yes from me when it comes to taking adventures with you and Poppy." She stood on her toes then and kissed him, feeling safe and held by his arms and even more so by his heart. He was so constant, so unwavering in his commitment to her, to her dreams, to her freedom, and to whatever they were building together, and she knew they were in for a very beautiful life together.

Author's Note

♥ ♡ ♥

Thank you so much for joining me for Meredith, Adnan, and Poppy's story. The final installment of the "Cats of Istanbul" series, The Wedding Scratcher, is coming soon!

To stay updated on other works in progress, please visit my website at kcmccormickciftci.com.

If you loved this book, please consider leaving a review, as that is one of the best ways to support indie authors like me. Reviews left on major retail sites (wherever you bought this book is a great start!), Goodreads, and BookBub will help other readers discover this book, too.

About the Author

KC McCormick Çiftçi is an English teacher turned romance writer. She spent the majority of her twenties living and working abroad, collecting the experiences that inform the stories she tells. She enjoys telling multicultural and international love stories through romantic comedy and women's fiction. She lives in Turkey with her husband and a herd of cats.

Prior to diving into the world of romance, KC published two self-help books for intercultural couples, *Loving Across Borders* and *The K-1 Visa Wedding Plan*. Both are available wherever books are sold.

For updates on upcoming releases, behind the scenes news, and all my favorite book recommendations, visit kcmccormickciftci.com (or just point your phone camera at the QR code below).

Books by KC McCormick Çiftçi

Austen in Turkey

Pride, Prejudice, & Turkish Delight

Sense, Sensibility, & the Mediterranean Sea

Home (Abroad) for the Holidays

Christmas on Inishmore

Christmas at Terminal One

Intoxicated by You

Intoxicated by You

Cats of Istanbul

The Vet Upstairs

From Strays to Soulmates

Intercultural Relationship Self Help

Loving Across Borders

The K-1 Visa Wedding Plan

Milton Keynes UK
Ingram Content Group UK Ltd.
UKHW040829041124
450710UK00010B/96

9 798988 901044